Before he knew what he was doing,
he had taken her into his arms. It just happened. And she stayed, one second, two, three. He kissed the side of her forehead, just rested his lips on her skin, not a real kiss, not what he wanted to do. As if she knew and wanted it too, she lifted her face to his, and he brought his mouth to hers. Holding back, trying not to tear into her mouth with all the passion moving through him, he kissed her soft lips, slicked with a hint of summer rain.

She had been huddled inside his arms, but now her hands slid around his shoulders, and she was holding him like she used to, pulling him closer, kissing his mouth open, still soft, still sweet, but yearning for more. She felt it too, then. He knew she must. He would not be signing those papers because she would not be leaving town. He just couldn't let her go. Not again.

Another clap of thunder must have brought her to her senses because she put a hand on his chest and pushed him away with the lightest touch, as if she were as reluctant to release him as he was to let her go.

"Want I should drive you home?"

They were inches apart, and their eyes held each other, telling stories neither would say aloud.

"Okay." Her eyes shifted to her bare feet, toenails painted peachy-pink something. His Courtney always wore black nail polish. This was somebody new, but she was also the same.

"We can sit and talk for a while, see if it slows down." He wasn't sure if he meant the rain or his madly beating heart. Maybe both.

D1524505

Praise for Cynthia Harrison's
Blue Lake Series

"[In *LUKE'S #1 RULE*] I loved the character of Chloe who puts her children first and, despite her love for Luke, won't let him treat her as second best."

~*Ali, A Woman's Wisdom*

~*~

"I cried three times while reading [*LUKE'S #1 RULE*], they were good tears, and I knew it would somehow all end well."

~*Nikki Carrera, Nikki Carrera Author*

~*~

"[*LUKE'S #1 RULE*] would be enjoyed by anyone who likes a contemporary family drama, slightly edgy, with a bit of romantic, sexy stuff thrown in, in the form of Luke, the man with the rule he's so determined not to break…"

~*Terry Tyler, Terry Tyler Book Reviews*

~*~

"*BLUE HEAVEN* wrapped me up and didn't let go until I finished the final chapter, blinking my way past tears in order to make out the final words."

~*Melissa Snark, The Snarkology*

~*~

"[*BLUE HEAVEN*] captivated me right from the start and I couldn't put it down. In fact, I read it in one sitting, ignoring everything else on my 'to-do' list."

~*Barb Han, author*

~*~

"Harrison has a wonderful tale [in *BLUE HEAVEN*] to tell in a great setting…an enjoyable light summer read."

~*Georgia Rose, Georgia Rose Books*

3/2016

Dear Vernie
I treasure your friendship!

Love and Death
in Blue Lake

⅗ thanks for the title ♡

by

Cindy

Cynthia Harrison

Blue Lake Series

Love and Death in Blue Lake

Cover Art by *Angela Anderson*

The Wild Rose Press, Inc.
PO Box 708
Adams Basin, NY 14410-0708
Visit us at www.thewildrosepress.com

Publishing History
First Champagne Rose Edition, 2015
Print ISBN 978-1-5092-0475-5
Digital ISBN 978-1-5092-0476-2

Blue Lake Series
Published in the United States of America

Dedication

For Ben & Owen

Chapter One

She walked in the door, a slice of light from outside illuminating her curvy frame. His Courtney had never gotten Hollywood skinny, even after all the years she'd lived there. She was like an angel. Glowing. Her heels clicked across the old wood floor as Eddie stood motionless behind the bar, soft cloth and a half-polished wine glass held loosely in his hands until he felt the glass start to slip. Then he gripped it too hard, and before it shattered, set it down on the bar. He threw the polishing towel over his shoulder and watched her walk to him, acutely aware that they were alone but at any moment another customer could walk through the door.

He hadn't expected her. The last time he saw her, she'd been wild with grief and he'd been drunk. Back then, summer of 1994, they'd been young and out of their minds in love.

They had a fight, then she was gone. She'd left behind all her baby doll dresses and chunky-heeled strappy shoes, left with nothing but the clothes on her back and big dreams he had known next to nothing about. At least this time he'd been prepared. Or thought he was, remembering the rough punch to his gut when she walked through the door of his bar.

He'd known she was coming in for the twenty-year Blue Lake High School reunion; the town buzzed with the news. This was the woman who had styled rock stars and designed lush video shoots with exotic animals and abundant food and outrageously frocked pop stars. To him, all this time later, she looked like his same sweet Courtney, but without the smile. They hadn't said a word to each other yet.

She took a seat at the highly polished wood bar and slapped down a large-sized legal envelope, thick with pages that spewed out the open top. No. Not after all this time. She wouldn't.

"Hello, Courtney."

"Hello, Edward."

She was the only person on the planet who called him that, and her voice with the name took him back in 1992 and their wedding day. He thought his heart would bust with love for his little rebel. They had to be together, more than high school sweethearts were allowed to be in Blue Lake, so they waited until they were legal, told nobody, and married at the courthouse in Port Huron. So they could live together and make a life, the life they'd been dreaming about and talking about and wishing for since freshman year of high school.

"Divorce papers?" He nodded his head slightly in the direction of the packet.

"It's time."

Her heart-shaped face hadn't aged a day. How could that be? And those deep rose lips, slicked with gloss. For him? He wanted to kiss her, not divorce her.

"You getting married or something?" He knew about the kid. Not his. She was, what, fourteen now. Scarlett. No, Ruby. Like the belly ring Eddie had bought for Courtney on their wedding day. Because they could never be like everyone else. And that's why…oh man, he hadn't thought about her or any of this in a long time. He knew how to block that shit out. And not by drinking. That worked for a few years, but then he got the bar and just stopped. Saw too many drunks, he guessed.

He took up tai chi and did the discipline that filled his head with nothing but the next movement in the flow. It worked…until now. Now he remembered that she'd begged him for a baby, but he thought they were still too young, and they didn't have any money, and he didn't want a hand-out from her folks. Also he was still trying to be a real musician then. He still had dreams of his own then. And they didn't include any babies. Courtney had tried for a year to talk him into it, but he kept saying no, and it broke something in her, and she left.

"Yeah," she said, like divorce papers after twenty years were no big deal. "Got any Chardonnay worth swilling?" She pointed at the half-polished glass. It was that time between lunch and dinner, between beach and dancing. He still had her alone. But for how long?

He took his time finding just the right bottle. Blue Lake had become a destination vacation for people with boats who loved big water and knew about wine, so he'd had to educate himself in the last few years. He'd even had a wine cooler installed, maybe just for this day. He opened the wine without flair, held the cork, looked at her. She shook her head but took the bottle from him to study the label before he could pour her a taste.

"Go ahead. Nice choice." He poured and thought about getting another glass for himself. It wasn't like he never took a drink. Just not at work. And he was always at work. "Now I'll just sip this while you read that, and you can sign before the shindig Saturday."

"We've been married for twenty years." He said the first thing he could think of, anything to stop this from happening. "You could at least give me the weekend to think it over."

Before she could take a sip of wine, she slapped a hand over her mouth, then laughed her same laugh, the one that tinkled and was throaty at the same time. God, Court, don't do this to me. Because once again he was back, this time 1993, the first time she brought up kids. It was after they'd gone at it until they were senseless and his bones had felt like jellyfish. He held her and kissed the side of her face. "Never thought much about having kids," he confessed. Hell, they were still kids themselves.

"But you want them, right?" She pulled away a little to look at him.

"You're still the joker, I see." Present again. He thought fast. How to make her stay? How to burn the papers in his big stone fire pit out by the river?

"It's so good to see you." He came from the open-heart thing the tai chi guy always yapped about.

She lifted the glass, but then didn't sip, instead setting it down, looking right into his eyes, getting a read, she used to say. She swallowed. He could watch her neck for ten hours and not get bored.

"Good to see you, too, Edward."

Ah, she'd softened a little. Her hand went to a small stone around her neck. An unconscious twist of gold chain and he glimpsed a little chip of deep ruby red. Not pierced in her belly, but still a part of her. Relief, hope, sadness tumbled through him.

"Tell me about him. My rival for your affection."

She snorted. Another cute habit that would fling him back to the past if he let it.

"Still with the words, too, I see. Do you play? Here?" She swiveled in her stool toward the big side of the building he only opened summers, with the stage and the dance floor.

He felt dizzy. This was not good, seeing her like this. Too much. All at once.

"You answer my question, then I'll answer yours." Lame, but it bought him time. Her wine level looked untouched. Probably not the right year or the right grape or something. He'd seen her sniff it and set it aside. Like she'd set him aside.

"Fair enough. His name is Xander. We've lived together for six years. He's the only father Ruby's ever known. He doesn't like it that Ruby and I are Fass and he and the boys are Stein."

"The boys?"

"Your turn."

"No. No place." He didn't elaborate, and he saw that she wanted to ask him more but decided not to. There wasn't anything to say. He quit playing guitars and started playing with women the day after she left town.

"Ten and twelve, from his former marriage. We're a family. He wants to make it legal. Have a child of our own. I said yes."

Eddie glanced at her ring finger. No rock. And she "said yes" not "I want that, too."

"Do you love him, Court?"

The door opened, and a group of twenty-somethings straight from the beach tumbled into the dark cave of his bar like a litter of puppies.

While he checked IDs and served the kids, she walked out. Tight jeans hugged her butt, swaying over the highest heels this side of Chicago. The boys in the group looked at her, still dead sexy. She didn't look back, just waved her hand. As he drew a pitcher of beer, he noticed she hadn't touched her glass of wine.

****

Courtney hoped Edward had not seen the way her body shook when she left the bar. She had not been prepared for the full force of Edward Calvin Fass aka Fast Eddie. She thought she'd been ready but had been in major denial mode. She still wanted him, damn it. She pressed the ignition button with a shaking finger and peeled out onto the highway. She drove with the window down, like it could blow away her thoughts, the ones that clung so tenaciously.

Think of Xander in California, she told herself. Think of your life there. Her practice. He'd been her prof and advisor at UCLA when she went for a degree after dressing up rock stars got old. Nothing happened between them for the longest time. He was married, and she was studying too hard to become a life coach for any thought like that to enter her mind. In California, they took things like life coaching seriously. Still, Xander, as her academic advisor, talked her into doing cognitive and behavioral therapy training as back up credentials. It would lend her gravitas, he said. Then he arranged for her to get the hundreds of hours of supervised practice such licensing required.

When she graduated and got certified, she took Ruby and moved to San Diego. She'd had it with L.A. With her savings from the days when everyone but she blew their money on blow, she started private practice and did just fine. Then Xander showed up six months in with a suitcase in his hand. He never left. Not that she'd minded. Not really. And things would straighten out soon. She pulled into the driveway of her parents' enormous porched and pillared home.

Her parents didn't know much about Xander. She didn't tell, and they didn't ask. Ruby had never really warmed to Xander, called him a mooch because he didn't contribute to the household. She parked in the garage the way her father liked and thought about Xander's other house, the one in L.A. with the wife and sons in it, the one that took all his money, the one where he sometimes spent weekends still fixing doorknobs and such. Some weekends he stayed in Beverly Hills and other, less frequent weekends, the boys came down. Ruby ignored them, and they didn't even see her, just ate up two weeks' worth of food in two days, food Courtney paid for, and didn't say thank you. Not ever.

Things were about to change. Big time. That's what this weekend was about. Xander was going to make the split final and tell the boys. They were going to be a real family, southern California style. As if he could read her mind, her phone pinged with a text. She stood outside the house and read "Picked up ring today. Want to rush to Michigan to put on your finger."

Courtney endured a family meal with Ruby, her sister Gwennie, Gwennie's twins, aged twelve, her baby brother, Kyle, and her parents. Sunday roast on a Thursday. Courtney had not eaten beef in years, and Ruby was vegan, but they both took a small slice and pushed it around their plates, under a bite of mashed potatoes, behind a few cooked carrot slices. It's what they did when they came to Blue Lake.

"Everybody says you were at Eddie's today for hours." Gwennie smacked her lips.

"Maybe an hour." Courtney shrugged.

"Is he my real dad?" Ruby asked, even though she knew he was not. Even though Courtney had shown Ruby the papers from the sperm bank where she had been purchased.

Kyle made a turkey baster joke.

"Kyle!" Mom's neck turned red. Dad, deaf without the hearing aids he refused to wear, and no clue of the subject, asked did anyone want more beef.

"Sorry." But before Kyle held out his plate for another slice of cow, Courtney saw the pleasure he took in the twins' snicker. Really, they knew that stuff at twelve now?

It went on like that until Courtney claimed jet lag and went to her room.

Courtney woke hours later, her daughter snoring softly in the twin bed next to her. The pine trees in Blue Lake were bad for Ruby's allergies. She could never move back. Not that she wanted to. Well, except that she'd been dreaming of Edward and of doing just that, but dreams were not wish fulfillment, they were more complicated. Just like her own life, her own hopes, fears, and desires.

Quarter after three. Edward would be home now. She knew where he lived. Gwennie had told her that and way too much more information about how he was the town man-whore and chose a different summer woman each morning, noon, and night. He had a special cottage at that newish resort, Blue Heaven, also a sofa in his office at the bar, where he'd disappear with them for an hour or two.

Courtney tried not to think, just breathe. But the room was stuffy, and panic started to rise. She padded into the bathroom for a Xanax but instead put on those jeans, the only pair she owned, bought specifically for this trip. She grabbed her messenger bag with the extra set of divorce papers and slipped out of the house. She forgot to wear shoes, but by the time she noticed, panic was pulling hard.

Her old bike was still in the garage, and she rode it out to Sapphire River Road, feeling her heartbeat stabilize and thinking back to just when these panic issues had started. She had been so strong when she was young. Strong with Edward, strong when she moved to L.A., strong when she forged a career in an emerging field, strong when she'd had Ruby on her own. The first time she remembered feeling panicky was in college. She had not been sure she was smart enough, even though UCLA thought she was. She'd hated the way her voice shook and her hands trembled when she presented in front of classrooms. For the first time, she had felt out of her element, out of control. She had shaken those episodes off for years until she wrote her master's thesis on the anxiety/panic/phobia epidemic. She'd come up with that one after Xander had nixed many other ideas. He had loved it. The more she researched, the more she recognized herself. College was as unfamiliar to the old Courtney as the moon. Funny, she'd always enjoyed new experiences before that one. But nothing, not rock stars, not motherhood, shook her confidence like an A minus.

She passed the canoe rental place and kept going

on the rugged dirt path. There was an unpainted open wooden gate across Edward's property. Like an invitation. She rode in and felt the kind of serenity she had been yearning for for years. Here was where she felt most herself. Here was where she belonged. She breathed in the feeling. If she could bottle it, she'd make a fortune. Edward sat very still in a lawn chair facing the rushing river.

"I've been waiting for you," he said. "That's why the gate's open."

She hadn't asked the question, but then Edward had always known her mind, sometimes better than she did. She noticed there was just the one lawn chair. A light rain started to patter against the leaves of the trees dotting his land. Probably in the light, it was a pretty piece of property. She could picture it because they'd been back here all the time when they were kids. Making out rolled up in a blanket by the river. Except now, behind them stood his house of glass, lit low from within. It beckoned her.

"I just came for the papers."

"Left them at the bar." He got up from his chair and took her hand, pulling her toward the house. The rain started coming down a little harder, so she let him lead her inside.

He opened the door for her. To their small world in high school, she'd been a rebel, a crazy one, but to Edward she had always been his lady. And she loved that. Their private world nobody would guess. Pizza and soda pop, not heroin and weed like some people said. Those kids didn't know them at all. She and Edward liked it that way. He drank a little with some other guys who played guitar and drove their cars fast down the straightaway outside town. Her outlet was scouring vintage clothes from thrift shops. She had an eye for design; it had given her a career. A way to leave Edward and this town behind. A way to have a child.

What she hadn't known then was that without Edward, she and Ruby, so in love with each other as only mother and newborn child can be, were lonely together. Everyone in L.A. was a player, so except for work, Courtney didn't go out much. She didn't want her daughter to have to deal with a merry-go-round of men. She loved her girl more than the world, but just not more than Edward. Ruby and Edward were meant to be her family, but somehow it never happened.

And somehow, when Ruby was four or five, Courtney forgot about him. Was over him. Wasn't interested in saying hi when she came home to Blue Lake. All this memory in a flash as she walked through the door of his home. It was a jewel box of stars and night and glass and wood. This was no typical Blue Lake abode. She'd seen some unbelievable places in L.A., but this was something else. She was in awe.

"So little Bobby Bryman did this as his Master of Architect project?"

"Yep."

"It's awesome, Edward."

"Thank you. The design was my idea."

"Well, now that you don't play guitar anymore, I guess you need some other outlet besides selling beer." It was a mean thing to say, and she didn't know why she'd said it except that her sister had needled her with the way Edward prowled. So stupid to feel a stab of jealousy after all these years.

The kitchen and living area was one big room, and

Edward made no reply as he walked to the fridge for a glass of water. "Anything?" He held up a second glass.

"I'm good."

"Sweetheart, you're better than good."

"Aw, now you're just proving my sister right."

Edward didn't miss a beat. "I know what people say about me. I don't care. That's why I have a glass house. I don't bring women here."

"But you have your own cottage at Blue Heaven. And a special room at the bar."

He hooted at that. "Gwennie doesn't have enough to do with twins? She has to make up fantasies about old Eddie?"

She wished she hadn't been so open with him, but that's what he did to her. No secrets. Never could keep anything from him. Impossible to start now. "Did you sign them?"

Edward drank down the entire glass of water there at the sink before he answered her. "No, I did not."

"Why?"

"I was busy."

"So why not now?" She whipped the other set of papers from her bag, walked toward him, slapped them on the sink. Then she handed him a pen. Or tried to. He didn't take it from her.

****

"I will sign the papers before you leave town. You have my word. Just not tonight." Truth was, Eddie shook so hard he couldn't hold a pen if his life were at stake. His heart slammed against his chest, over and over, like a punching bag. She was so beautiful. Barefoot in blue jeans. He wanted to hold her more than he wanted to breathe. On the outside, he stayed calm, inside he was afire.

Lightning ripped the sky in a ragged fork, and the rain beat down harder. She jumped at a clap of thunder, and before he knew what he was doing, he had taken her into his arms. It just happened. And she stayed, one second, two, three. He kissed the side of her forehead, just rested his lips on her skin, not a real kiss, not what he wanted to do. As if she knew and wanted it too, she lifted her face to his, and he brought his mouth to hers. Holding back, trying not to tear into her mouth with all the passion moving through him, he kissed her soft lips, slicked with a hint of summer rain.

She had been huddled inside his arms, but now her hands slid around his shoulders and she was holding him like she used to, pulling him closer, kissing his mouth open, still soft, still sweet, but yearning for more. She felt it too, then. He knew she must. He would not be signing those papers because she would not be leaving town. He just couldn't let her go. Not again.

Another clap of thunder must have brought her to her senses because she put a hand on his chest and pushed him away with the lightest touch, as if she were as reluctant to release him as he was to let her go.

"Want I should drive you home?"

They were inches apart, and their eyes held each other, telling stories neither would say aloud.

"Okay." Her eyes shifted to her bare feet, toenails painted peachy-pink something. His Courtney always wore black nail polish. This was somebody new, but she was also the same.

"We can sit and talk for a while, see if it slows down." He wasn't sure if he meant the rain or his madly beating heart. Maybe both. "I'll still drive you. Can throw your bike in the back of my truck." Eddie didn't like talking and especially not that many sentences in a row. He waited for her to turn him down.

"Okay."

That was the girl he knew, always easy with him, going along, well except for the baby part. She went along with everything until one day she didn't, and no matter what he said, he could not change her mind, and then it was too late and she was gone.

He took her hand and pulled her to the sofa. She let him. He held her hand a little longer than he should have, and she pulled away first.

"There was only ever you for me." What had he just said? And how could he take it back? "So you love him?" He tried to cover his declaration with more words. "The way we loved each other?" He had to know how she felt. Because he was feeling caught back in time, caught back in her.

"So, what? No sex for eighteen years?" She folded her hands in her lap, demure as all hell, her gaze leveled at her fingertips, which he noted were painted the same shade as her toes.

His little vixen, acting so innocent, but with the quick retort, sting in tail. "Well, none that meant what we did."

Her soft laugh was just the same. She moved with slow grace, hugging her legs to her chest, refusing to look at him. Or answer him. "All the girls in school loved you, and I'm sure they formed a consolation line the minute I left town."

"I was inconsolable." Sure, he'd gone through those girls in a matter of weeks, but he wasn't proud of it. After that first dazed year of sex and anger that turned into a steady stab of sadness, he slowed down, yeah, he still fooled around, but he never loved. He didn't bother with excuses, he just walked. Way he saw it, women knew what to expect when they took him on.

"It doesn't do any good to talk about it." Forehead pressed to her knees, voice muffled.

"No, I suppose not, but why should that stop us? We always could talk about anything." And then he remembered that it was true. He could always talk to her. Ten sentences in a row. Hours of talking and dreaming and loving her. The cracked window inside him opened wide, and it all rushed back in, as fierce inside his body as the weather outdoors.

Her head came up as if she felt the shift in him, and she turned her face to his. Her eye makeup had smudged in the humidity. She used to do that on purpose, like a sexy vampire. He reached out and touched her face. "Your eyes…"

"Oh god." She tried mopping up the mess, but made it worse.

"No, don't. I like you like this."

"Yeah, 'cause you're crazy."

"About you. Your eyes always said come here and love me. They're saying it now."

****

He kissed her again. And she let him again. This time they went a little rougher, let their hunger out a little more. She slid against him, and his hands roamed beneath her damp shirt. That caught Courtney. What was she doing? She was engaged. She was happy. She was living her dream life. Or so she thought, until she'd seen Edward today. This was crazy. How could everything change in a matter of hours like this? It

15

couldn't change. She wouldn't let it. She was divorcing Edward and marrying Xander. End of story.

She pushed him away again to catch her breath. "I can't do this. I'm sorry. I still love you, I'm always going to love you, but we have new lives. Good lives. We have to honor that."

"You're still my wife, so if you mean cheating, technically you're cheating on me with him."

"Then I guess you've been cheating on me a lot."

They laughed like they used to, and the years tumbled away. He pulled her up and toward the loft. She let herself be led up the stairs even though the rain had stopped, the clouds had cleared, and stars were visible through the skylights. He pushed her down, just a gentle touch, but she knew what it meant. They'd done this before. A lot.

"Edward. We can't." She sat up on the bed and looked around. She'd wanted to see his personal space, that was all. Or that was what she told herself. What she saw was that the rain had stopped and the first pink of dawn lit the sky.

Edward must have seen it too. "Damn if that sky doesn't match the color of your mouth."

She remembered wearing bright red lipstick when they were together in public, but in private she always went soft for him. Could he really remember a detail like the exact shade of her mouth? She felt his hot gaze, saw him twist his neck to watch her over his shoulder. She sat on the bed, her purse open, a tube of glossy tint, that yes, she picked it up and saw he was right, matched the dawn which came super close to her natural lip color. She felt unutterably sad. It was the weirdest thing because she had only recently gotten everything she ever wanted. Hadn't she?

"I'll throw your bike in the trunk." His step down the stairs was fast and sure.

"Don't bother." And she was down the stairs and out of the house even quicker than he could move.

"Court, honey, there's no need to be upset." He caught her hand and held her in place, looking toward the more blue than green water of the Sapphire river, engorged by the recent deluge. "Friends?"

She sighed. It occurred to her that she still loved him with all her heart, and that fact broke her resolve. She squeezed his hand. "Yeah. And more. You'll always be in my heart. But that's the only place you have in my life now." She bit on the side of her thumb until she remembered she gave up that nervous habit fifteen years ago. "You can drive me home. I have to tell you something, anyway."

She watched him swing her bike easily into the back of the truck. It was the only way to stop this. She had to tell him about the baby.

Chapter Two

Courtney didn't want to tell Edward about the baby. She had been slowly realizing that her feelings for him had never gone away. They had hibernated. She didn't love Xander. She didn't want to raise a child with him. She didn't want Ruby to be Xander's legal daughter. She wanted all of that, but with Edward. How had she been so blind?

He wasn't going to go for the baby. Not if he was the Edward she'd known so well.

"I don't know how to start, so I'm just going to say it."

"It's like we never went away, isn't it?"

"All those feelings just rushing back." She let the warm night air hold her close. She was with him again. Her one love. She shook herself. She had to come clean. "Damn it, Edward, now wait. You don't know everything." She wasn't angry at Edward; she was angry at herself for letting her heart feel these things they should not be feeling. It wasn't gonna work. No way. Sure it felt right, but so did heroin, from what she'd heard.

"I don't have to know everything. I just need to know one thing. Do you still love me?"

"Yes." This was only making it more difficult. "But there's a problem."

"Ain't no mountain high enough…," he sang. He

used to sing for her sometimes.

"I'm pregnant."

"Baby?"

She wished he was calling her baby, but she knew he was asking the big question. The one that had seemed so happy and right before she began planning her return to Blue Lake and started thinking about Edward again. She put her hand on her belly. "Yep. Nobody knows. Not Ruby. Not my folks."

"He know?"

"Yeah. He knows."

Edward drove without saying anything. She waited for the accusations disguised as analysis for a few minutes before she remembered that it was Xander who did that, not Edward. Edward didn't have any degrees to flaunt. He just had songs. He didn't make her feel small the way Xander could, all the while sounding perfectly logical so that she, a trained therapist, became confused when Xander started in on her. Was he manipulating her? Was he just sharing his wisdom? She never knew. Ugh. A lifetime of that? What had she been thinking? Maybe she could have the baby and just stay here. See what happened with Edward. Suddenly it seemed the only answer.

"Well, I hope you're happy." When Edward finally spoke, she heard the clog in his throat. What in the world had happened to them, and why did it have to stop before it could even get started?

"I am, but I wish it was yours."

"Oh God, not that again. What are we doing? Repeating history?" Edward played it straight. She could always count on him to say what was really on his mind. And if he wasn't sure, he didn't say anything until he was.

"I know. Edward, I'm sorry. It's just happened maybe six weeks ago. It wasn't planned. But I found out, and well, you know how I've always wanted..." She didn't have to finish the sentence. They both knew what she'd always wanted. The one thing he'd never wanted to give her.

"So now he wants you and Ruby all legal and sewn up. And he has the perfect prize. Better than any precious gem."

That had been, until just hours ago, the truth of it. "He's still married, too. He's been living with me, but neither of us ever got around to the paperwork, and his wife needs him. She doesn't have a job. She relies on him."

"Huh. So, then, this baby, it's not legally his until you put the name on the birth certificate. We could stop this truck right now and do the things we used to do, and then this will be *our* baby."

****

Eddie couldn't believe the words that had just come out of his mouth. But she sighed and took his hand. Her hand was so soft.

"You don't mind that it's his?"

"I...listen." He needed to make like a bicycle and back pedal. Fast. They didn't call him Fast Eddie for nothing. "I don't know what to think. I love you. It's like you said. It all came back like you were never gone, like I got a do-over, and I won't lie, I wanted one from the minute you walked into my bar. But babe. I have never thought one minute about ever having kids. And marriage? I'm married. We're married. That's my thoughts on marriage. My wife lives in California, and I have not seen her in eighteen years. It's gonna take some time to wrap my head around all this."

"Well, that's why the divorce. We can still do that. We'll get a divorce, and I'll marry Xander…" Why was she saying that? Letting him off the hook so easily?

"If he in fact divorces his wife. Sometimes they don't. I wasn't planning to."

"You weren't?"

"Nope. I was gonna take my shot with you. I was gonna see how this weekend went, and if it went the way I thought, I was gonna ask you to stay. I mean, not move in or anything right away, but you know, date."

They both laughed, breaking a little bit of the tension Eddie felt. Married twenty years and dating. Only them.

Then he parked the truck in front of her folks' house, and it really felt like high school. He turned to her, his eyes full of unshed tears. "Shit," he said.

She blinked, and a few drops fell from her own eyes. "I know." She wiped the tears away quickly, impatiently. This was not tear and tissue time. This was brass tacks.

"I have to ask," she said.

"Go ahead. Not sure I have an answer."

"You said you were going to, like past tense?"

"Oh, damn, you know I hate grammar. But okay I get it. I had a plan, and now that plan has a wrinkle in it, and I shot my mouth off about raising a baby that isn't even mine but belongs to some geezer out in LaLa Land, and listen. I need a minute. Okay?"

Well, okay. She wasn't going to say she wanted the baby and him and Ruby to be a family. She wasn't going to say dating first for a while seemed right. She wasn't going to say anything. She was giving him permission to think about things. This was a big fat complicated mess. He'd worked hard to simplify his life since she'd gone. Now in a matter of hours she'd thrown everything into disarray.

Eddie got out of the truck and unloaded Courtney's bike. He kicked the stand down and left the bike there on the sidewalk. For some reason, she was still sitting like she was glued or something to the seat of his truck.

He opened the door on her side and light flooded the cab of the truck. They stared at one another. She put her hand over her mouth, let out a tiny gasp. Eddie forced himself to stay silent, to not ask "what?" He moved to one side, and finally she slid out without saying a word.

He opened his arms and held her. "I need to think about some things," he said again. And then he took both her arms, moved her away like a chess piece, and walked around the road to his side of the truck. He got in and drove away.

****

Eddie seemed damn happy to Bob Bryman. Man loved his bar. He'd told Bob once that it was perfect because he didn't have to think about anything but serving his customers. Eddie tapped a beer and set it on a cardboard coaster in front of Bob, who was waiting for Lily. She was late. Lily was always late. Not that they'd seen each other much since he'd gone to architect school and she'd gone off to learn videography. Bob was thinking of an earlier time, when he'd been with Lily every day for an entire summer. He wanted more than anything for this summer to be the same, except better.

"Thanks, Eddie. House hold up okay under the storm last night?" Bob was proud of his first work as an architect, and would not have asked the question, would not be in the bar but at the site, if he didn't already know the answer.

"Tight as an enchilada rolled from Tomas Sanchez's own hands," Eddie confirmed.

Bob nodded. "Good to hear." But really, he didn't hear, not really. He was too busy thinking about Lily. They had kept up a sporadic connection through college. He refused to go on Facebook, but she found him on another site he frequented, a group of M.Arch. majors. Like a little detective, she found him, and from there they emailed once every month or two. A few texts, fewer calls, never anything personal, except once she said she'd been considering becoming a lesbian. Could you do that? Decide?

He'd always thought sexuality was determined by DNA, but he looked into it a little deeper and found that it wasn't quite so simple. Some women had such bad experiences with men that they deliberately crossed over. But then, after a few months, Lily mentioned a guy. Then another guy. Many guys, never the same one twice.

Eddie set another beer down. Bob hadn't realized he'd drained the one in front of him, so busy had he been looping round and round his non-romance with Lily. Except she seemed, the last few months, warmer. Called him sweetie, for one thing. Bob pulled out his wallet before he remembered the deal.

"Your money's no good here. You built my house, and that's that," Eddie said, not stopping to chat. Typical summer evening and the place was hopping.

Here came Lily, looking lovely as she ever had, not one day older, and not a bit like a lesbian, whatever they looked like, which had to be because they looked like everyone else, far as Bob knew.

"Hi, sweetie!" She kissed him. On the lips. Before she scooted her barstool closer to his and sat down. Eddie was there in a flash, and she pointed to Bob's beer. "Same." Eddie poured the beer pronto. "And could I have a shot of Stoli?"

Eddie brought Lily's shot in a pretty little glass. The kind his brother's wife liked to buy at antique stores. That's how Bob met Lily, because of Eva. Lily was not from Blue Lake. She had blown into town, a teenaged runaway who worked for Eva, Bob's sister-in-law, at Blue Heaven. Then he and Lily went off to different universities, and his brother Daniel and Eva got married and made Bob's childhood home into a place of their own. Blue Heaven was now run by a staff, and Eva had taken over the bachelor pad Bob had grown up in. That's just the way it was. He'd had five years to get used to it.

Lily slammed down the vodka and batted her eyes at Eddie, asked for another. Eddie obeyed with alacrity. So it wasn't just him, Bob thought. All men were putty in Lily's hands.

Now he totally understood about Eva and Daniel. Bob had only been home a few weeks, and he already needed to get out of there. His brother and Eva kissed all the time. In front of him. They chased each other down hallways and up stairs, and Daniel grabbed Eva's ass once when he didn't know Bob was coming around a corner. It was truly excruciating to witness. He'd be that way with Lily, if she'd let him. God, he'd been so lovesick back when they were kids that summer.

After Lily had two vodkas and a half beer, she turned to him with a brilliant smile. "How's Eva?"

"She says hi." There was a red flag waving in Bob's head he was trying very hard to ignore. Meanwhile, Lily finished her beer and put it on the ledge of the bar like a regular. Eddie filled it with a big smile.

"Hey, you're the gal doing the reunion video, am I right?"

"Yes," Lily said, not looking away from Bob.

Lily videotaping the reunion? This was news to Bob. Wait. Maybe Daniel had said something about it last night. Bob had been busy thinking about Lily then, too. She'd texted asking to meet at Fast Eddie's tonight, and he had thought of nothing but this moment since reading that text.

"One more for the road?" Lily asked.

Eddie had kept the vodka bottle close and poured out a neat shot. That gave other people ideas, and soon Eddie was lining up lemons and sugar and vodka shots down the bar. Bob also noticed only Lily got the special glass. He wondered where they were going next. Dinner? The bungalow at Blue Heaven? Lily had texted that she was staying there. Eva only let friends and special customers stay in her bungalow. Eva loved Lily almost as much as Bob had. She'd missed her too, but then Eva had Daniel and Bob had nobody. Now here Lily was, wearing short shorts and a tight sleeveless shirt, showing way too much skin for such a dive bar, no offense to Eddie, but really, the place was a burger joint with a band.

Lily clicked her fancy glass to Bob's beer, and they

drank up.

"So you want to go out for some dinner?"

"Oh no, I'm not hungry. Are you? I'll have another drink if you want to get a burger."

"No, I'm good." Bob couldn't eat if Eddie pulled a filet mignon out of thin air. "He won't let me tip." Bob whispered this in Lily's ear, so as not to call attention to his special status. The Brymans had special status in town anyway. Everybody looked up to Daniel and looked out for Bob, but the tourists didn't know that.

"Then let's go!" Lily jumped down off her stool and almost fell off her sandals. She grabbed his arm and steadied herself.

He looked down at her long legs. Her sandals had some sort of rope-thing for a heel. They made her calves look really good. The red flag in his head waved again. He ignored it as they walked to his car. But while Lily sang along to the radio at the top of her lungs, Bob remembered something Eva had said about Lily having some kind of issues or something with a guy back home. "Lily will tell you when she's ready to," Eva had told him before she and Daniel had driven him to college. Lily had never mentioned "home" not even once. She talked about classes and a guy named Dean who was teaching her to shoot a gun and certain cinematographers she admired as if he knew who they were. He'd looked them all up, even Dean who was an old guy, an ex-cop. Bob never asked why Lily wanted a gun. College campuses were scary for some women, but Lily was back in Blue Lake now, and if Bob had his way, she'd never leave again.

****

Lily left Bob in the bungalow's living room, her

hands shaking. She could do this, seduce him. She just felt a little dizzy from drinking all that vodka. She checked her purse, but the gun wasn't in it. She unzipped her hard shell black and white polka dotted suitcase: business cards, video equipment, gun. Her clothes were still in the paper bag where she'd thrown them when she'd left home. She had not taken much, only the essentials. She grabbed her gun, secured it in the lock box, put both in the drawer beside her bed. There was not much she'd wanted from home, not much of anything she'd kept from college. What she wanted was a fresh start and a true confession. And she aimed to get both.

She didn't know how yet. She had a half-formed plan. It needed an accomplice. Maybe Bob, if she did it with him. But her relationship with Bob was so pure. She really loved him. She thought of Eddie. Would he help? Could she even explain? He'd always been kind to her. And there had to be a reason people called him Fast Eddie.

She felt, however irrational, that her cousin was coming for her, she was next on his hit list. He'd killed her mother, he'd made her seem like a kook to her father, which didn't take much convincing, and now he owned her family company. But she, like her mom, was a loose end. She shivered. Loose ends got clipped. Steady, she told herself.

Her cousin didn't know she had a secret weapon: Dean. Dean, the retired cop who had trained Lily how to shoot a gun straight and true. All the years she shot video, she also shot target practice. It made her feel safe to have a gun because her cousin was a ruthless son of a bitch.

Everybody said her mom's accident was just that. A tragic accident. But her mom loved her Caddies and took scrupulous care of them. She was the world's best driver. It was no accident, but Lily only had one way to prove it. She had to get a taped confession out of the bastard. She called Bob into the bedroom. What the hell. She'd had just enough vodka to live dangerously for a night.

A knock on the bedroom door. She peeked through a crack, and there stood Bob. Looking as good as he ever did and scaring the hell out of her, because she wanted the security and safety of him, but she had to get him to do just the opposite.

"Lily." He stood there with that same stupid look of adoration he always wore; it made her heart sing despite everything. But her heart hammered too, like big drums in a small band. She threw herself at him, and he caught her.

"Oh Bob," she said. His arms tightened around her waist, and she burrowed in deeper.

Bob's arms felt like home. She buried her nose in his neck, thinking about what she'd just done. How to extricate? Panic was already rising. Damn. She'd been through this with her therapist. She wasn't even a virgin. But with Bob, she felt like one.

She pulled away and grabbed his hand, tugging him onto the bed. Then she told him what had happened to her mother. She left out the parts that hurt too much to talk about. She left out the parts that would scare him. She'd already secured her weapon. She liked it better in her pocket, but for now, she was practicing courage.

Before long, they were making out. It always

happened like that. They'd start something she couldn't finish and predictably, it went the same way this time. Like a bad rerun of a terrible sitcom.

She started to cry. God she was sick of being so hung up because of that sick bastard. Bob looked worried. Of course he did. He never wanted to hurt her. He never would.

"Just screw my brains out," she said through tears.

"Lily!"

"Well." She wiped her face on her shirt. "I love you. You know that. I want this. You know that, too. I was raped, okay? And it happened just a few days before I met you, back when we were just kids, and that's why all the drama. But I'm over it."

Bob put his arm around her. "Honey, I'm not sure you are." He moved her hair to the side, kissed her neck.

"Wait." She had to tell Bob the rest before they could do it.

She just had to have one person in the world who believed her or at least pretended to, and if she told him he had to believe her before they did it, he'd say he believed her. He'd waited five years for her. He'd do anything. She'd always known that, and it was her safe place. It wasn't like she took advantage. Well, maybe a little bit.

She took a breath. "So do you really want to?"

"Only since the first day we met."

"There's just one thing," she said. "Before we…you know."

Bob looked up at her from where he knelt on the floor, placing his shoes just so. It broke her heart a little bit, the way every sweet thing about Bob did.

"What's that?"

"I have to tell you something, and you have to believe me." She pulled her shirt over her head, so he could see her pink lace bra.

"Okay," he said. She felt him go into complete silent attention. Like he was studying really hard for an exam.

She unzipped her shorts to give him a peek at the matching panties. Then she got up and unbuttoned his checked cotton shirt. Freshly pressed with light starch. He was perfect, and she was about to wrinkle him. She hung the shirt on the bedpost.

"Are we going to be naked when we talk, because..." Bob's voice sounded parched. It was sweet the way he so sincerely cared. He sort of worshipped her. Would it be enough? It had to be!

She pulled back the duvet and sheets and light summer blanket. An answer and an invitation. He quickly shed his jeans and got into her bed. She kept her underwear on because guys liked that stuff.

He knew her so well. Knew to prop himself on pillows, his erect penis modestly covered by the sheets. She hadn't even caught a glimpse of it. Such a gentleman, her Bob. God she loved him and she hoped after what she had to tell him he still loved her. She reached over him to get the gun.

****

Lily in pink underwear was spectacular. Lily in pink underwear holding a gun was stunning. She'd just demonstrated her ability to lock and load like a criminal or a cop. She'd explained about Dean, her cop daddy. He got all that. She was afraid of rape on campus. She was afraid of campus shootings in general.

He nodded, his stomach twisting like one of those soft pretzels they sold on the beach snack shack.

As crazy as her story was, she handled her gun with a professionalism that made him feel confident. She slid it back from where she'd taken it, into the night table drawer, inside a lock box. Good. Then she said, "I need it to get my cousin to confess that he raped me and killed my mom. I'm going to hold the gun on him and film his confession."

Bob had lost his erection the minute she'd pulled the gun from the drawer. He never thought she was going to shoot him, well, maybe for a split second, but she had not pointed it at him and he'd settled down, that image of her, gun across her heart, burned onto his brain. He didn't think too much about the stir happening in him again. She was damn hot. He was only human. But maybe there were issues here he needed to understand, hard-on and all. With another part of his mind, he thought that if it was anyone but Lily, he'd already be the hell out of there.

"Your cousin killed your mom? Like on purpose?"

"Yep. See, she believed me about the rape. It was a real sore spot between her and Dad because he believed my cousin. They were close. Are. He always wanted a son, and I'm not a guy…" Her words were slowing down, even slurring a little bit.

All that vodka finally catching up to her, he'd bet. Bob's ribs could barely contain his beating heart. What she'd been through. What she wanted to do. "What can I do?" He was in. He might be sorry at some point, but right now he had to help his sweet sad girl.

He ran a hand over her pearly skin again and took her into his arms. Her breasts mounded against his chest and he let his hands move over her in what he hoped was a strong yet comforting way. "I'm so sorry about your mom. When?"

"Christmas. Just after."

"You never said."

"I was having a hard time. I still am, but I'm seeing a shrink, and like I said, I have a plan for justice."

Bob didn't utter another word. He just held her and stroked her hair. His poor Lily was more damaged than he had ever imagined. He wanted to avenge that. It burned in his gut.

"What happened is he tampered with her car. She loved her car, and she was an excellent driver. Now you know that four-way stop on Highway 15?" It was a flashing light. The only one for a stretch of miles. "Well, there's an old utility pole on the right, just past the crossroads. And Mom, according to witnesses, blew through the light, swerved to miss another car, and crashed into the pole. Killed instantly."

Now Lily was crying. Bob felt her tears run down his chest. He held her tighter, questions forming, logic asserting itself.

"So what I need from you is to tell me there is a way someone could tamper with her brakes so that nobody would ever know. Her brake lines were not cut, nothing was wrong at all with the car. But he did it. I know he did."

Bob might not be a cop, but he needed to know some basics. Who these witnesses were, and where had the cousin been, and how he had conveniently planted a car at that intersection. A convergence of unlikely events at the very least. Still, he'd work with the assumption that she was right. She needed somebody on her side and that person was him. She'd chosen him. So he'd get answers to questions like the road conditions. It had been winter. Could have been ice. So many questions. But he wasn't going to ask Lily, not right now. Just now she needed comfort and to know he was on her side. Questions would only upset her, and right now she needed someone to believe her. He was going to be that someone. Because he loved her and because he remembered something a mechanic buddy had told him once.

"So then, do you believe me?"

"I do." He believed she believed it, anyway.

She stumbled out of bed, plucked a box of tissue from her dresser, and he got the full view of her long legs and full breasts. God, he wanted her. She blew her nose—hell even that seemed sexy to him—and dove back under the covers, cuddling up to him. He held back his anger at the cousin, but some of it came out in the way he grabbed her and held her tight against him. His fingers lightly dug into her tender skin. He kissed her

"Do you believe me? Or do you just wanna do it?"

Lily's voice sounded as if she'd chugged a bottle of wine in six minutes. Her neck was at an odd angle, but she didn't seem uncomfortable. He moved her head onto his shoulder and held her there, feeling like he was literally holding her together.

"No, honey." He kissed her forehead. "I got a buddy, he told me you could add a bottle of water into the brake fluid, and the heat would do something to make it sink down below the fluid and evaporate, but not before it rendered the fluid ineffective. By the time the cops show up, the water is gone. No evidence.

Unless a really good inspector catches it. Sometimes they do and sometimes they don't."

Like a beautiful doll come to life, Lily reanimated.

"Well, this inspector is best friends with my cousin, so I'm thinking he didn't notice a thing." She climbed on top of him like he was a mountain. Moving slow. The vodka. But she smiled when she felt how hard he was for her. She rubbed against him, and he moaned. The thin cloth of that last layer between them tormented his entire being. Her head fell against his pillow; her lips touched his ear. She let out a giant snore.

Bob sighed, carefully cradled her in his arms, put her in a comfortable position on her own pillow, then covered her with the light summer blanket. He got out of bed and dressed. He sat on the edge of the bed watching her sleep for a long while, then finally, when he was sure she'd be okay, because she tossed and turned and snored and muttered in her sleep, he went home.

He got in his car and drove and as the radio blasted out "I Bet My Life" he wondered, could what they'd come up with—this crazy scenario—be true? Or were they both just spinning stories? And what about her plan with the gun and the filming? She'd need a second person. Was all this just a plan to seduce and enlist him? And would it work? He just didn't know. And he didn't know anyone he could ask. Unless.

He didn't know where else to go, so he turned in when he got to Fast Eddie's place. The neon light that shone down from the top of the barn-like structure when the bar was open was dark. The smaller neon light with the same hot pink and blue colors as the big sign when it was turned on, the one that said OPEN, was also dark.

Bob checked the dash clock. Yeah, the place had been closed for hours. The sun would be coming up any minute. He made a fist with his hand and took knuckles to his stiff neck. Too long sitting staring at one place, one woman. He used to think that when he built his first house, he'd become a man. Now he knew he'd only really be a man when he saw Lily through this mess. The gun. The confession. He had to step up. And he had to do it alone. She was the only woman in the world he'd do something like this for—it wasn't about sex—it was about protecting the woman he loved.

Chapter Three

Courtney stood on the sidewalk lacing up her walking shoes, thinking about Edward and how they'd left things this morning. It had all gone from wonderful and impossible to just sucking in minutes. She was confused and sad. The shrink needed some therapy, but all she could think to do was undress and wrap herself in her soft childhood blanket. She slept for several hours, the jet lag catching up with her, then had dinner with the family before deciding to take a solo walk around her old neighborhood.

She passed Doc's old house, so many memories of cuts and bruises and once or twice a broken bone being set in his house, which had also been his office. A For Sale sign was hammered into the lawn and by the looks of it, had been there awhile. Not many people wanted a big red-brick four square. Most new buyers liked the cozy 1950s cottages. This was a place for a family. Her family.

With Courtney, it was all about following her strong intuition. Every good move she'd made had been through her own actions. Every bad move had been instigated by someone else. Like when Xander had showed up on her doorstep and moved right in without even asking. She'd been flattered at first, grateful for the companionship second, and then just sort of settled in. But it had been wrong. It had not been her choice; it had been his. She could fix that. It was time. In fact, well overdue. Even if she just kept this place for a vacation spot, a get-away, just stayed the summer, she wanted it. She had her own money, and the San Diego house was a rental. She wanted a home. Here. Now. It felt right.

Even though it was way late, the sun had not quite set, so Courtney took out her phone and called the Realtor.

He apparently wasn't too busy because he came right over with a key.

She had no idea what she was doing, but in her mind she thought about color and chintz and decorative touches like carved cornice boards that would make the Bryman school of architecture, even Bob with his glass and open design, gasp. Courtney loved color; it made her happy. And stars knew she needed some happy.

"Is it okay to videotape you? I'm trying to get historic footage to include in the reunion video." These words startled Courtney, and she turned to spy a wisp of a girl who appeared out of nowhere the minute the Realtor—"Call me Spence"—showed up with the key to Doc's place.

Spence the Realtor, no last names needed in Blue Lake, Courtney remembered, gave the girl with the video camera an aggrieved look. Then he said to Courtney, "Daniel Bryman said she could follow people around a little bit if she wasn't too intrusive." He gave the girl one more hard look, which she ignored, filming away. Courtney shrugged. Permission granted.

"Doc died ten years ago." Spence got out the key and unlocked the door, blocking the threshold. "His kids kept this as a summer place until a year or two ago." Spence pointed out the diamond windowpanes and the mellowed timber porch. Courtney loved it. It cast a spell on her. She was too old to be a princess, but she felt enchanted. How would Ruby feel? Well, as she'd rationalized, they didn't have to stay. Not forever. Not right now. But this would be her refuge. Waiting for her whenever she wanted it, even if that was not until Ruby was in college.

"You interested in using this as a residence or a commercial property?" Spence the Realtor asked.

"Both. Maybe. I'm not sure."

"So you're a doctor?" They had gone through the big foyer with the staircase into the front parlor. Pocket doors sealed the room from the family's domain. She didn't need medical doctor stuff in here and pictured a library office with bookshelves behind a sofa and comfortable chairs and her desk. Through the pocket doors, in what could be a dining room, she'd make a cozy family space with a television set where she and Ruby could watch movies and the baby could play. They crossed to the kitchen. An old farmhouse sink was still there, but nothing else. Lots of room for a dine-in kitchen table. A blank palette. Her favorite thing. Light slanted in the windows.

"So what kind of doctor?" Spence asked.

"Cognitive and behavioral therapist."

"No shit!" The video girl put her camera down. "I could use an emergency appointment."

Courtney snapped out of her whatever it was, some kind of dream where she stayed in Blue Lake and practiced in this house. Just to see what would happen with Edward. That fast, everything seemed over with Xander. Her life was moving at warp speed. She had her first patient but hadn't even been licensed by the state yet.

She told the girl that.

"Could we just have coffee? I'm away from my shrink for the first time in five years, doing this job, and I really, really, really need advice. No meds, just someone to talk to. Cognitive therapy. That's talk, right?"

"Right." Courtney saw the way the young girl's hands shook.

"Please. Oh, I'm Lily. You can ask the Brymans about me." The Brymans were the town's most prominent family and good friends with Courtney's folks. "They know me. I used to work for them…"

Spence took Courtney's elbow. "Young lady, get your footage, and then you and my client can talk after she's seen the rest of the house."

They did a walk through of the upper floors, and the house was a solid Bryman structure. The first Bryman had been an architect who designed many of the historic homes in the town. It had been built in the 1930s, and like so many of the homes in this town, by one of their own, only recently brought to national prominence by the youngest generation of Brymans. There would be no need for repairs or retrofitting. Ruby's room, nursery, her bedroom. The bathroom had a gorgeous Victorian tub and a pedestal sink. Perfect. God, this was confusing, but some parts were very clear. She wanted this house. She'd hire someone to watch the baby in between clients. Keep her list low.

There had been moments in Courtney's life, not many, but a few, where suddenly a light showed her a path, and it was clear and certain. This was one such moment. She felt dazed by the clarity of it. This was her home. She was sure of it.

It was very close to move-in ready and decorating would be a pleasure. "I'll take it." Courtney heard herself say the words, but she didn't quite believe them. She'd have to ask her mom for a down payment unless Spence would take an out-of-state check. She realized with a jolt that her lease was up on the San Diego house next month. Just another sign. Xander did not approve of "signs" or anything else smacking of the Jungian. Well, too bad. She didn't have to live with his silent disapproval anymore.

Spence gave her his card, and she promised to come by his office in a few hours. She felt happy, then terrified, like she'd been in a car crash and hit in the head by an air bag and pink fairy dust was flying in the air all around her. But it felt so right, she refused to worry.

Lily sat cross legged on the wood floor, waiting. When he learned who her folks were, and had scanned her license and credit card, Spence had given Courtney the key. He shut the door behind him and Lily said, "I'm going out of my skin."

Thank stars for yoga, Courtney thought, lowering herself to the floor across from Lily. "We're just talking. This is not a session."

"I don't care about that. I need to unload, you're qualified, hell you just bought your office. Should I put that in the video?"

"I don't know." Courtney tried to bring herself out of the pleasant daydream daze and into a more professional persona, but it just wasn't happening. "I guess that would be okay."

"I'll interview you for the reunion video later. First I have to tell you what happened to me and my mom. My thing happened a long time ago and I had a ton of therapy about it, was getting over it a little bit, but then the same guy who raped me just killed my mom, like at Christmastime. Last year. And nobody, not even my *Dad*, believes me. Also, he's my cousin. The murderer."

****

Lily left Dr. Fass in a great mood Thursday night and woke up Friday morning feeling fine. In a way, Lily felt like a spy. Her life was something she preferred to keep blank, all the easier to fall into other people's stories. Now she had a story, and it was a nightmare. So she was taking a little break from it to film this reunion, and bam, she meets a therapist. The perfect therapist. It was like when she met Bob. When she met Dean. Everything was working, for now. She just had to keep it together until she could execute her plan.

Fast Eddie from the bar had agreed to let her film his hermit cave. Because of the Bob connection. A total honor. The therapist had the same last name as Eddie. Were they cousins? Married? Dr. Fass did not wear a wedding ring. Lily had checked the footage before she began filming the Sapphire River. She'd never even known it was back here. The big lake was the main attraction, unless you knew about the Sapphire. It was wide and high, and its waves chopped and churned.

Eddie had promised to meet her, and she kept filming the water until she heard his truck turn up the road. She had a mystery to unravel. The mystery of the Fass connection.

"We need to do this fast. I have a business to run." Eddie was already at the door, letting her into the glass house. Oh well, she could shoot exteriors afterward.

"Hey, you know what's funny?"

He seemed not to hear her.

"I just had an appointment last night with a Dr. Fass. Are you related?"

"Courtney?"

Lily shrugged. "Yeah, I guess. You related?"

"We used to date in high school."

She filmed the downstairs, all one big room. All glass. Big panes of glass. Bob was amazing. If only she could love him the way people in songs loved each other. Body and soul. Some kind of magic spark. But she loved him like a brother. She'd never loved anyone any other way than the way she loved her mom. And her dad, when he was still Papa. And Dean. Dean she loved like a dad, but Dean was gone now. Or she was gone. She wouldn't go back to the college town in southwest Michigan. What for? She had a new therapist right here. And this therapist would teach her how to love Bob properly.

Eddie walked up the stairs, so she followed, wondering how to ask him for help. She had a feeling Bob would need a backup. Someone older and smart. Like Dean, but she wouldn't ask Dean. They'd said their good-byes, and she had to stop relying on him. It was time.

"You two seeing each other again?" She couldn't bring herself to ask for help. Not yet. She had to do this reunion job first, then take care of her personal shit. High school sweethearts reunited. Would make a good story for the video. Eddie had always liked her, calling her Ms. Lily when she was just a girl, only seventeen, and blew into town on her way to somewhere else, destination unknown. She liked that sense with her work too—who knew what she'd uncover? This was her prelude to uncovering a murderer.

For the video's sake, she would find out the real story of Eddie the mystery man, and why he and Courtney had broken up, and how they got back together. Because of course they would. They didn't just date. They must have been married to have the same last name. And Dr. Fass had not changed hers, so she never remarried. Made a nice little happy ending for the reunion video. Her next video shoot, the one featuring her cousin, would not have such a happy ending, but she was okay with that.

She filmed the top floor of the engineering marvel Bob had designed. She interviewed Eddie, who'd had his hair trimmed for the special weekend. Maybe for Dr. Fass. She didn't ask, but she left her camera on after she set it up on the tripod, filming the inch of white that showed where Eddie's neck now met his hair.

She adored that the only sound was the whoosh of the river rushing into the background. The woods surrounding Eddie's property created a layer of hush. It felt like church.

Eddie made sure her lens took note of all the signature Bryman touches, updated for a new century and Bob's particular vision. Like her, Bob already had a vision.

"What would it look like in a storm like the one the other night?"

"Saw some lightning streak across the sky when I got home from the bar." Eddie pointed up at the skylights.

Lily dutifully aimed her lens up. Bob's design just kept on impressing her. She didn't know enough about his vocation. Guys liked when you asked them questions about themselves. Right? Bob. He wasn't just any guy. Her heart hurt. It felt like the organ, just a thing that kept her alive, wanted to escape her body and search him out. It yearned toward him. Snap out of it, she told herself.

Maybe she *was* in love with Bob. If that was true, love and work just didn't mix. All the more reason to work up her nerve and ask Eddie for help.

She looked for clues to unlock his cooperation, but there was nothing to see, not even behind her camera. A bed. A table with nothing on it but a lamp and an iPad. That was it. A walled off space running the length of the room was off limits, he said. "My closet. My bathroom." That's all he let her in on. She was intrigued by the things inside drawers. Inside backpacks. Inside medicine cabinets.

She'd missed the telescope at one of the windows. Filmed that. Okay, three pieces of furniture, four if you count the lamp. This guy took minimalism seriously. She put her camera down and peeked into the telescope. She saw the village of cottages and then, closer to the water, the bigger Bryman homes in the rich section of town, where Courtney's family lived. She saw the canoe rental place closer up and the empty acreage that went on and on because it was not on the water, but across from it. She saw the Sapphire like a ribbon running through it all.

She filmed for two hours but was not satisfied. She wanted behind the bedroom door. Maybe his guitar was in there. Everyone talked about how he once had a shot, how he wrote such great songs. Bingo, bet he wrote them for Dr. Fass, bet he stopped when she left him. Why did she leave him? Lily would find out. She wanted to disappear into their story and leave hers behind, if only for a little while.

She reminded herself she wasn't ready to speak to Eddie about her problem just yet. First, she had to talk Bob into helping her. Then, together, they could convince Eddie that nobody would get hurt if they did it right. But Bob might need a lot of convincing himself. And she would need a lot of therapy in order to do that part of it. Okay, first things first. Did she need to make a list? Mind on job. This job, not the next one.

****

Spence said he'd rather have a check written from the local bank. He also said he could not move a sale as quickly as she'd requested, but he had permission to execute a temporary "rent to own" so she could move in anytime. Courtney's mother handed over the money, no questions asked, huge smile giving away her happiness. Courtney, still in a state of disbelief in her actions, went to the bank and deposited the money. Then she went to the real estate office in town and signed the papers. Edward was coming out of the dry cleaner, pressed checked shirts slung over one shoulder. He looked up at the sign, although everyone knew Sanchez's was next to the real estate office and always had been.

"Buying property?"

Suddenly she felt dizzy and clutched a lamp post. What would it mean to say yes, what would then come after? She'd been gone too long. This was not her home anymore. She loved her life exactly as it had been.

Before Edward kissed her. Hadn't she?

He was at her side in two steps, his hand cupping her elbow.

"You okay?"

"I bought Doc's old place. I might be losing my mind."

"Oh that. No, you've always been a little nuts."

Edward, always with the joke to deflect from the serious situation at hand.

But then he got serious. "Is it the baby?"

"Oh, no, I don't think so. But maybe…" She thought it was very sweet that he cared about the baby. If only it was *his*. God, he was right. She was a little bit nuts. This was happening way too fast.

He had told her almost nothing about himself, but he knew everything about her past, present, future. He had followed her career, told her so. But would he let her in? Would he say one thing about the music or why he didn't drink anymore or a special woman? Maybe there wasn't one. Maybe nobody, not even she, got in. Her fault? Maybe. He'd asked her for four days, but that was before the baby.

She stood, shook him off.

"Sure you're okay?"

"Yeah, oh yeah, I'm fine." Her phone chimed. A text. She checked. California.

"See you later, then," Edward said. And before she could stop him, and why would she anyway, he was gone.

Seeing Xander's name, she knew. He was not The One. Edward was The Only One Ever. Damn. Her eyes swam with tears as she blinked to read his text. Something about how much he loved her.

She didn't reply. She'd just bought a house. Spence had promised to fast track the sale. The family needed the money. Even if the paperwork took time, she had the rent-to-own agreement and could establish residence sooner that way. How long until she could get her license to practice here? She had to find out. Make it all legal and right.

Courtney got in her car and headed toward Port Huron. She needed a bed. Two beds. It was time to stop sharing a room with Ruby in her mom's house. She'd tried to find her daughter earlier, but her mom said she'd taken off with her guitar. Courtney looked toward the beach and punched in the line for Ruby's cell.

"I bought us a house." Courtney heard the waves in the background. Ruby was at the beach. "Where are you? In town? By the park? Do you have a cover up? Flip flops?"

"Mom, what? A house?"

"Maybe we need a vacation place. A place of our own."

"Yay!"

"So you want to come furniture shopping with me?"

"No, I'm, um, I have a thing. I'll pick out some stuff online and send to your phone, okay?"

"Okay, but what is this 'thing'?"

"Grandma said it was fine."

"That's not an answer."

"I'm taking guitar lessons, okay?"

"Oh." Courtney thought for a minute. Edward would not take on Ruby. Never in a million years. "With who?"

"Sorry, Mom, my battery is, like, dying. I have to

find those pics to send you. Do *not* choose a bedroom for me!"

The phone went off, the radio went on.

In Port Huron, she found a furniture store and picked out stuff, including things that looked close to Ruby's pictures, asking for Monday delivery. "Not a problem," the guy said, taking her credit card.

At dinner that night, her folks were beyond pleased that she was moving back to Blue Lake. Gwennie had heard the news and brought over a huge stack of shelter magazines that the sisters went through after dinner, Courtney picking out paint colors and ripping out pictures of furniture and appliances. Ruby shrugged when Courtney asked how she liked the retro-looking kitchen appliances in one of the magazines. "Just get us in there, so I can finally get some rest. You snore, Mom!"

"I do not!"

Nobody said anything about Xander. He'd never even tried to get to know her family. Never came for a visit, even at Christmas. It was like he didn't exist here. It felt so easy to erase him.

Ruby asked to be excused. "I'm going to call Juanita and tell her every single thing to pack."

"Hold on, honey. You don't want to go back to San Diego for school?"

"Naw. I think it would be cool to start over here. Or did you forget I start high school this fall?"

"No, I didn't forget…I just…" Now was not the time to mention the baby. "Won't you miss Xander? Your friends?"

Ruby snorted. She tossed her hair and left the room.

"Come back." Courtney jotted a quick list and handed it to Ruby. "For Juanita. This stuff too."

Her mom and dad had finally finished the dishes and came to sit in the front room with their daughters.

"I'm calling movers to come in, box, and ship. Just have Juanita get everything together when Xander's in L.A. this weekend." She would have to call him first and tell him that he could stay in the San Diego house for one more month and then the lease was up to him. She would not be coming back. What would he say about the baby? He'd been pleased when she took that pregnancy test and it came out positive. But they hadn't discussed financials, and that was huge. She didn't want to continue to support him while his ex-wife lived in over-medicated splendor in Beverly Hills.

"So when I start high school, it will be here." Ruby was back, assuring Courtney that Juanita had it under control. "I told her we'd give her excellent references and a big bonus."

"Good thinking." Courtney felt that now she had her family's blessing, she must surely be doing the right thing. Ruby had wrapped her head around the new situation with aplomb that belied her age. Courtney hugged her daughter. "I'm so glad you're taking this so well. It's really cold here in winter." All talk of "vacation home" had disappeared. They were staying. Courtney felt as if she were escaping from a life she had never really wanted. Xander had been the one who had moved in on her six years ago. No invitation necessary. She'd been living a version of her life another person had created. Not that it had been a bad life—she'd done very well as a life coach with impressive credentials—but this was her own vision. A new start.

"Are you kidding?" Ruby jumped up and down with irrepressible enthusiasm. "I can't wait for snow!"

Courtney knew she'd have to tell her parents and her daughter about the baby, but that could wait a day. Or two. After the reunion on Saturday.

Her mom was saying that she and Dad had talked it over and wanted to have the house painted for her as a house-warming gift. They knew a painter who could use the work. Courtney handed over the color swatches she and Gwennie had collected.

****

Eddie left the dry cleaner and was getting into his truck in the town lot when he'd spotted a girl who could only be Ruby on the beach, flirting with some older guys who were pretending to admire her guitar. They weren't local, and their eyes were not on her guitar. He felt immediately protective, knew at once the girl with the guitar was Ruby. She was California sun-tanned with long shiny dark hair when every other girl on the beach was a pale blue-eyed blonde.

Courtney had been on his mind, he'd just seen her, spoken to her, and now here her daughter was, getting into trouble. Apparently, Courtney didn't realize that the town had changed since they were kids, and that fourteen-year-olds had, too. He hung his plastic-wrapped clean shirts on the truck hook and went down to the beach, taking the guitar from Ruby and asking the guys if they knew she was only fourteen. They left soon enough.

"Why'd you do that? My grandma's at the hair salon. She said I could come down here for an hour. Just because you're married to my mom doesn't make you my dad." She grabbed for her guitar, and he gave it back to her, stunned she knew about him. Recognized him.

"Oh, uh, I didn't think, well, Ruby, I'm Eddie."

"My mom calls you Edward in her journals."

"So that's how you know we're still married?" This girl was all Courtney as far as attitude. He liked her sass. Some of that had gone out of Courtney and into Ruby. Or maybe it was just the age. "Your mom would be pissed if she knew you were reading her diaries. She didn't even want me reading them." He'd forgotten all about how Courtney wrote back then, just scribbling, she called it. He'd never looked. If she wanted him to know something, she'd tell him. When she'd left, she'd taken the diaries with her. And apparently she'd kept them all these years. "Anybody else know? Your grandparents?"

"Xander." Eddie nodded, but Ruby, lost in thought, didn't notice. "My mom doesn't know I know. She doesn't know I know anything. Except we're moving here. She told me that. But not about the b—uh, anything else."

He figured Ruby didn't need to know he knew about the baby. It was hot in the sun. He was used to being behind the bar this time of day. "Well, if your grandma says it's okay, I guess you'll be fine. It's just…tourists. Until you get to know the locals, people aren't gonna be looking out for you."

"How'd you know me?"

"Your mom showed me twenty-five pictures of you on her phone."

Ruby nodded. "Hey, will you give me lessons? Some girls I was talking to said you teach people how to be musicians. Like, real ones." She strummed a few chords to that old song "Ruby, Ruby," but she didn't sing any words, just grinned at him and said "Hey, hey," at the perfect time with sweet clarity. Girl knew her roots.

Eddie liked that. She had talent; he was willing to bet on it. But he could not get involved. "Sorry, kiddo. I don't think your mom would like that."

"She already said it was okay."

Eddie doubted that. He just shook his head and walked back to his car. "Careful now, you hear?"

****

Eddie watched his staff handle shift change. He'd offered the bar for a party tonight. All graduates from the nineties, not just his class. He had free drink tickets for them, a buffet full of food, a hand-picked band. Extra staff were at the moment being organized by his manager. Amid all this Ruby walked in and sat right down at the bar. She put her guitar on the seat next to her, like it was a third person. The two live people stared at each other across the thick wooden barrier for a few minutes.

"My grandma dropped me off. She said you better give me lessons or your name is mud in this town."

Eddie laughed. If Courtney's mom said it was okay, then he surrendered. He'd always admired that woman and never been intimidated by her. Now Courtney's dad was another story, but that was ancient history. The man had mellowed from all accounts. Not that he ever set foot in Fast Eddie's. He shook his head at Ruby as a smile couldn't help twisting up his face. "From the sound of it, you don't need to know any chords."

"I don't. But I want to try out for *American Prodigy* next year, and I need stage presence. Grandma says you teach that kind of thing. Plus you gotta say yes cuz I figure besides me, you are the most important person in my mom's life. She's been different since we got back. We're staying, you know."

Eddie took that in. He wondered if it would really happen or if this Xander guy would lure them back to the land of never-ending sunshine.

"Your grandma know about the baby?"

"I—I shouldn't have said that." Ruby blushed. Maybe he could teach her a few things about what emotions to let out and which ones to conceal. Fans wanted happy confidence, not nervous tension.

"No, don't worry, kid, you didn't. Your mom told me." He didn't know why this girl got to him. She looked like him, hell, she even had a part of him, a younger version of himself with her musical ambition. "And your mom says it's okay, about me taking you under my wing?"

"So, that's yes? You will?" She'd placed her guitar on the stool next to hers.

Again, he wished she was his daughter. Ruby laid it on the line. Just like her mom. Eddie was not used to doing that. People told him their problems. He listened. But Ruby didn't have a problem. She was making observations and planning for a future. She seemed far too astute for a girl her age.

"You want a cola or something?" By law, she shouldn't be sitting here at the bar, but he happened to be good buddies with the police chief in town, and the place hummed with a few locals and daytime drunk tourists, so he wasn't worried.

In response to his offer, Ruby made a rude noise, but he saw that it was fake, followed by a well-rehearsed line. "I don't drink that crap." Then a surprise. "Wanna get out of here? I need to see this glass house you live in."

"Absolutely not. I always give lessons here at the bar. You learn stage presence on a stage." He nodded toward his state-of-the-art platform. Then he rethought his words. She was underage. In a bar. Maybe not the best environment for Courtney's daughter, or anybody's daughter, for that matter. "Oh hell." He didn't like all these people coming to his house, which for all that it was built of glass was still in the middle of nowhere, his solitary sanctuary. But what was his choice? Say no and see those eyes fill with tears? "Okay, yes, under one condition. Call your grandmother and tell her where you're going."

She hopped off the bar stool, took out her phone, and walked toward the stage, speaking into it clearly enough so that he knew she was really on the phone with Courtney's mother. Where Courtney was, he had no clue. And he wasn't going to ask.

Chapter Four

"Wow this is awesome." Ruby slowly twirled, taking in the big room with wide-eyed wonder.

Eddie thought about Xander. The guy was crazy to let Ruby and Courtney out of his sight for one second, let alone an entire summer. Eddie had a million questions, but Ruby was a kid. It wasn't fair to ask her, so he swallowed the words stuck in his throat.

"I always wanted to meet you—even before I found out my sperm donor dad had like four hundred kids." Ruby the irrepressible. Said what she was thinking. So like her mom.

Eddie opened the fridge and poured sodas. The kind that were full of sugar and really bad for you. Ruby's eyes lit like sparklers. He'd had a feeling they would.

"I'm not supposed to," she admitted.

Eddie added a healthy shot of rum to his. He was not a drinker and contrary to rumor was not a former drunk. He just didn't think it was good business sense to drink much when you owned a bar. But he needed this one. Ruby was still staring around, her head tilting every which way, when she took the soda he offered and sipped.

She was elegant. Like Court. Every thing she did, every gesture she made, that deep twinkle in her shining eyes, Courtney, Courtney, Courtney. So he listened to her sing, and he gave her some tips, easy stuff, stand up, don't sway back and forth so fast, shoulders back, feel the music. Relax. Feel the music deeper. Keep the emotion genuine. She sang and sang, and he thought she had the sweetest voice and a nice way with the guitar. She wasn't flashy, but her deceptive simplicity was endearing and should be nurtured.

She could be his daughter. She was easy to like, same as her musical style, she was bright, sweet with a slice of lime. He went off on an imaginary journey of her high school graduation, then college, of course she would go to Harvard or at least U of M, walking her down the aisle for her wedding, holding his first grandchild, swaddled in a baby blanket. Was it pink or blue? His imagination failed him there.

"The thing with Xander is, she doesn't love him." It was like Ruby read his mind. "Not like she loves you. Or used to." This must be more gleanings from the diaries. "She doesn't know, and you better not tell. I think you won't. I trust you because I know all about you, plus I get that vibe." She came up for air, sipping her soda.

"Xander blew his stack when he found out she never divorced you. Even though he's still married! Mom never asked him to move in. They never had a thing when she was in L.A. He just showed up looking like a lost puppy dog, and she let him in. And he stayed. She didn't even ask me because I would have voted *no*. He doesn't even like me."

She set her empty glass on the counter and sat on a stool, propping an elbow on the island and cupping her face in her hand. "So now this wedding. It's ridiculous. She wants one more baby before it's too late. Hello?

They are both married to other people. He'll never divorce his wife. The wife gets half of his everything, which is not much. She's one of those stay-at-home types who can't cross the street without him holding her hand. He still spends time at her place, fixing faucets and whatnot. To see the boys. And he brings them to *my* house. I don't like it. But do I get a say? No. Xander's giving Mom the life she always wanted, except it's too late, and anyway she's doing it with the wrong person. I mean, Xander is harmless, but he's pedantic. That grates on my nerves just a little bit. Okay, a lot. Sure, we're a family in a California way, but in another way, I know my real family is here. With Gram and Gramps and Aunt Gwennie and the twins and Uncle Kyle." She took a breath and looked at him, and Eddie saw something vulnerable there behind the bravado. "And you."

"Pedantic. Now that's a twenty-dollar word." Eddie stalled, wished he didn't have to drink all that soda to get to the rum. This is what he did at the bar all day. Listened, nodded, poured drinks. The bar…Angry Angels…the party.

"Your mom is going to wonder where I am."

"Well, good. Maybe it will make her take a breath and think."

Eddie realized they'd been at this a while. A long while. "Don't your grandparents expect you for dinner?" He guessed he'd expected Courtney's mom would come over here and pick Ruby up, but he should have offered to drive her home before now. Time got away when music was the theme.

"I can hear the river," she said instead of answering. "The river was your special place until you got the apartment."

She had apparently memorized those teenage diaries her mother had written so long ago.

She had tears in her eyes. "I feel like I need to write a song. Something's too big inside, too heavy. It's gonna sink or swim." Her tears remained in her eyes, all shiny and unshed. His heart pierced. An arrow. "I don't blame you for not wanting a kid back then. You were right. The timing was off. She'd tell you that herself now." Ruby tilted her head toward the skylights.

"I have always loved the stars up here," she said, a few tears escaping down her cheeks. "I think we could have a good life here, and I think it's what she wants. What I don't know is what you want. Edward."

She pinned him with a look and struck an open C chord, loud.

I want Courtney. I want the three of us to be family, he thought. No. Four. Ah, shit, no. Too complicated. He stuffed his thoughts back down in the vault. He had a well of feelings and maybe writing a song wasn't such a bad idea. He wrote with his bands. He could write with Ruby.

"Okay. Let's write a song," he said.

The sweet relief on her face was reward enough for missing the first hour or so of his host duties. They wrote lyrics, nothing really stuck, but they had fun. They both loved Andrew Bird and he helped her work out "Lusitania." She could play by ear and sang the female part just right. She could whistle, too.

Hours passed until finally she said, "You know it's midnight?"

He hadn't known. Damn. He would be a horrible father. Or no, if he was her father, she was exactly in the right place. But he wasn't her father. So he sucked. Courtney must be so worried.

"My grandparents think my mom got special permission to bring me to the bar. Like I have to have a stamp or a wristband or something. I love music, duh. I might love it because of you. Let's go catch the last set. Want to?"

"Let's go." Like her mom, Ruby was a force of nature, and Eddie had lived long enough to know you just had to ride their wind.

****

Courtney loathed gossip. It was difficult to form a polite response to the second hundredth question *So do you have dinner with the Kardasians?* But she gave it a shot. "I don't live in L.A. anymore, and when I did those girls were in diapers."

"But didn't you help decorate that commercial for Paris Hilton?"

"I don't work in that field anymore. I'm a therapist now."

"Oh, too bad."

Once people got the idea that her life was not an endless A-list party, they started sharpening their knives. It was the same girls from school, women now, who just didn't know how to be nice.

"You waited a long time to go to college."

"Yes, but I wouldn't change a thing. I had my fun, lived some dreams, and now I'm helping other people live theirs."

"Huh. So a shrink. I heard you bought Doc's old house. Nobody here needs a shrink. Well, Spence had issues, but he's from downstate. That one is strange too." Someone pointed out Lily behind her camera.

"I can't believe you're leaving California for here. Is it because of Eddie? Are you two getting back together?"

Good question. She shook her head to clear the tumbled thoughts. Her mind felt like scrambled eggs. What had she done today? And where was Edward? The party, actually the pre-party, was at his bar, but he was nowhere to be seen. She hadn't seen him since she'd told him about buying the house. And he'd walked away. She wondered if she could live in a town with him and not be his wife. Would he divorce her now, when she finally admitted she loved him? She couldn't blame him. He'd never wanted kids. Except for maybe twenty or thirty seconds very early this morning when they'd both been sleep deprived and on high arousal.

"Is you daughter his?"

"She's fourteen. I left eighteen years ago. You do the math." Courtney felt immediately sorry she'd snapped, but people could be so rude.

"Yeah, but you came home a lot."

"I never saw Edward when Ruby and I came home." That was true. She'd stayed away on purpose.

"So who is her dad?"

"He's not in the picture."

"A rock star? From one of your video shoots?"

"She looks a little like Jimi Santori."

Courtney didn't respond. She couldn't stop thinking about Edward, about the fact that they both knew how they felt for that brief time and could hardly admit it to each other, forget about other people in this small town full of big mouths. She sipped her tea, the color of wine, in a wine glass, so nobody would question her not drinking. She hated all the questions, and that was just another one she was not ready to deal with. Soon enough, everyone would know.

Edward. Where was he? She's always been a self-diagnosed social misfit. She tended to panic in crowds of strange people. But Edward was a man she could talk to. They'd find a quiet corner away from all the small talk and cutting gossip about this one's weight gain and that one's wrinkles. She suddenly wanted to flee, but to where? Back to her family? She wanted to see Edward more than she needed to be alone. Would he ever admit he loved her? The playlist said he loved her with every single song. But she could be making that up. They were all from the year they graduated. 1992. But he'd slipped a few in from 1994. Her favorites. The band was good. She let the music take her and let the conversations around her float away. She heard someone say, "Courtney's drunk," and she hid a smile. People believed what they wanted to believe.

Then the band played the opening chords from a song from 1999. She'd done the video, one of her last. About the toxic chemicals between two people, she'd designed the entire shoot with Edward in mind, and that had been the song that had wiped the last vestiges of him from her life, wiped him away. Then Ruby came, and she was able to put him out of the picture, most of the time. He didn't belong there. How did he know? Did he receive her message, all the little things she'd included in the video so private to them, but disguised? Did he sit here in Blue Lake and watch and know?

I mean, really, it was the only song he played that was not something that had been in their collection, had not been from '92 or those few from '94. Where was he?

She wandered the barn-like room, smiling, saying hi, staying in slow motion. She wanted her photo albums. She wanted her car. She wanted her clothes. Her office furniture. Her notes. She wanted her clients to all come out and still be her clients, but that would not happen unless she set up an online practice. Like on Skype. People in her profession were doing that more and more now. Well, life coaches, not licensed psychologists. Either way, she had to establish a presence here. She would have new challenges. Substance abuse. Sexual abuse. OCD. ADHD. Not "where's my bliss?" She knew another therapist, a good friend, who would take some of her clients. She'd have to call each of them and tell a few of them that they were ready for life without a coach. And call her friend to ask if the referrals would be okay.

"Where's Eddie tonight? He never leaves this bar." A guy whose name she could not remember grabbed her arm, stopped her slow progress through the room.

"I have no idea."

"Lookin' good, Courtney."

Now she remembered his name. Joey. He used to taunt her because she didn't wear a bra. He used to make fun of her black nail polish and little dresses. He'd grown a beer belly. So many of them had. Yes, substance abuse. That would be her clientele, and they'd be hostile, coming on order from work or jail. Like this guy. It was enough to shake her to her bones. That was the social phobia. She'd be okay if she just took some deep breaths.

"You, too," she smiled and used all her strength to wrest his hand from her arm. Just then a girl from their class came up, glaring at Courtney. "Joey. Honey. This is our song." She shot Courtney one last look as she led a sheepish Joey away. "We've been married fifteen years. Hands off, bitch."

Well, okay then. Courtney pretended the over-processed blonde with bad teeth was a hostile client, even though she'd had very few of those. Her people came to her for answers to life's big questions. They wanted to know how to make things better. They had moved on from the flatline of high school. Some people never did.

Another guy. Captain of the football team. Still in reasonably good shape. A kind smile. He'd always been a nice guy. "Where's Eddie?" At least he tapped her shoulder instead of grabbing her arm. He leaned in to her a bit, because the music was loud.

She wanted to scream. Who was she? Edward's bodyguard? She shrugged and smiled. Lifted her empty glass of tea and went to the bar to refill.

She had brought a special bottle and stuck it in the cooler. People would talk about that, how she made herself so at home here. But it was for a reason. Mr. Football followed her. "You are lookin' good, but then I always had a crush on you. Even with your wild style."

Courtney didn't believe him for a minute, but was glad she'd poured the tea into a wine bottle. Something to do with her hands to keep them steady. She took off the stopper and filled her glass. "Gee, thanks." They smiled at each other. Checked for rings. He didn't have one. Neither did she. "Divorced. Jeannie Halsworth. Two years. We got two kids, boy and girl. You'd of thunk that would make it stick but nope."

Sounded like the divorce had been Jeannie's idea. Sounded like he knew she was a therapist. Once people found out, the troubled, the terrible, the lonely hearts, came out of the woodwork. But he stopped there. "You and Ed aren't still married? I heard a rumor."

"Just like high school all over again." She avoided the question. "Rumors all day and all night." She laughed. Shrugged again. It was the first genuinely happy moment she'd had all night. Edward was her husband. At least as of today. Until he signed the papers.

She felt herself start to sicken and excused herself, escaping into the bathroom. Social anxiety. She hated that label. She hated "shy" too. She was a plain old introvert, and parties were not her thing. Especially when sober. Especially when Edward had decided to disappear. She needed their world of two to feel safe.

A cluster of women shared a cigarette, and the buzz of their drunk conversation stopped the minute she entered the room.

"You tell Eddie we were smoking, and I'll yank your hair out."

God. High school just looped and looped again.

"Stop it, Char." Another of the group stood up for her. Surprise, surprise. "We were just saying how romantic it is, you and Eddie together again."

"We're not."

"We heard you're still married."

"It's complicated. I'm, uh, excuse me." She went into a stall and threw up. Sure, the women thought she was drunk, but she knew morning sickness when she felt it.

She came out and someone handed her the empty

wine glass. She'd been knocking them back all right. "Guess I better stick to water." She gave a feeble chuckle and rinsed out her mouth, using a disposable toothbrush.

Everyone laughed and that was that. Until…"Linda saw you. She's Mark's girlfriend. He owns the canoe business on Sapphire River."

Courtney felt queasy. She just wanted to leave and find some soda crackers. Edward probably had them in the kitchen.

"He doesn't bring women there. It's his hideout. But you were there last night. Really late."

She didn't have to say anything. "Excuse me," was the best she could do, slipping out the door as more people jammed in the bathroom.

She went into the kitchen, closed for the night, and found oyster crackers. She munched in the dark. Just a few. She should leave. But she wanted to see him so bad. Felicity found her.

"Why are you hiding out in here? You used to love to dance."

"Still do. Feeling a bit rough at the moment." She held up the individual-sized crackers.

Felicity's eyebrows raised, but she didn't comment. She didn't ask where Eddie was, either. It was after midnight. Would he even show? To his own party?

"You still live around here?" Courtney vaguely remembered Felicity. They'd been friends in grammar school, and then Felicity faded, just as everyone except Edward had.

Felicity laughed. "Brooklyn. New York."

The opening chords to *the* anthem of 1992 played.

She'd read it was about Kurt Cobain's girlfriend's deodorant. She didn't care. It had spoken to her then, it spoke to her now.

Felicity grabbed Courtney's crackers and tossed them on the counter. She grabbed Court's hand and led her out of the kitchen and onto the dance floor, even though this song was not a great one for dancing. It went from slow and dreamy to screamy, but Courtney knew every lick, every beat, every time she needed to move an arm or swing a hip, and so did Felicity. They grinned at each other, mirrors. Some of the class formed a circle around Felicity and Courtney and clapped along, giving up on trying to keep time to such a weird beat. Felicity whipped her long hair and Courtney did a slow shimmy, moving her body up and down to the chorus. How low—she'd show them how low she could go.

The singer looked impressed from behind his microphone. That used to be Edward up there. Now he mentored these kids, his protégés.

After the song, people laughed and clapped and the singer came down off the stage. "You have to be Courtney." He still had his mike clipped on, and the crowd roared with approval. Huh, tide turns. Courtney glowed, not from the praise of her classmates, but because Edward had told his band about her. In enough detail that they'd picked her out easily. Courtney laughed and nodded and introduced Felicity and slipped off to the sidelines. Too much attention always made her uncomfortable, and she figured it was time to go. She was all out of small talk.

Felicity came over after the singer got mobbed. "That was fun."

"It was. Thanks." Dancing was one way she lost herself. Didn't feel on display. Just felt her body in its elemental state.

"I have to tell you or I'll hate myself, but I always admired you when we were kids. You always knew what you wanted. You never compromised. You're the reason I moved to New York to pursue journalism."

"You are kidding me." Courtney felt confused. "I was the class joke."

"Not to me. And not to a lot of people."

"That was because of Edward."

"No, Courtney."

Felicity had always been scary smart. She should listen to her. "I wish you still lived here."

"Yeah, heard you bought Doc's house. Just for summer or full time?"

"I don't really know. It was an impulse. Honestly, I still can't believe it."

"Well, your mom is over the moon."

Felicity's mom and Courtney's mom were friends. That's how the girls had gotten to know each other as toddlers.

"Still a journalist?"

Felicity laughed. "No, not really. I freelance a bit. But mostly I'm a mom. That's why Brooklyn and not Manhattan."

Courtney heard the last word but didn't. Because Edward had just walked in the door with a guitar strapped to his back. And he was with Ruby. She had her guitar, too. And Lily was suddenly there, filming it all.

****

His staff, his regulars, his former school chums, all

wanted a piece of him, but Courtney was all he could see. She only had eyes for her daughter. "Ruby, where have you been?" She ran and hugged the girl to her, and the two of them stood whispering. Eddie snapped out of it and went back where he belonged. Behind the bar. Which is where he'd been when Ruby had ambushed him earlier.

His band, the guys he'd been helping get their act together, called out to him, and he had a faint awareness of the sound. The smells of the bar itself were the usual crushed peanut and spilled beer and sweat aromas that were like a heady perfume to his nostrils. But her. She eclipsed everything. Even with a thick wood bar between them. He went over, meaning to talk to the lead singer of the Angry Angels, but it was like he had entered her spotlight and now it was just the two of them on the barn wood dance floor, their gazes locked. Even Ruby drifted out of his consciousness for a minute, until he realized that's why he'd said yes to her earlier. Because he couldn't let go. Not of Courtney. It hurt to be with her, but being with Ruby was easy. She was so like Courtney. Ruby giggled at the lady from the grocery store, obviously drunk, who came up and said, "Oh how sweet, the little family reunited at last." Every word she said meant the exact opposite. That much was clear to Eddie. Courtney was about at the end of her patience. She was going to run out of calm in about two seconds. He tried to think of words to help, but Courtney surprised him. She turned to Ruby, said, "Behave," then took Eddie's hand. It seemed natural to lead her out to the dance floor.

From the corner of his eye, Eddie saw Ruby move his guitar case under a table and order what he hoped was a ginger ale from a server. After the dance with Courtney, he would take Ruby up on the stage and together they'd play "Lusitania." She had to make her public debut sometime, and Eddie thought she was ready. Then he remembered he hadn't played in public since Courtney left town eighteen years ago. No matter. She was in his arms now, and at this moment, that's all that mattered.

****

Courtney held on to Edward as tightly as she dared with all the eyes in the building trained on them, including Ruby's. She wanted to get mad at Edward and say he should have called, but she couldn't. He had his arms around her, and that's where she wanted to stay. Forever if possible. Could it be? Had he changed his mind? Would he be okay with her baby? It felt like it. Especially when her heart cracked open and out spilled a lifetime of love, right on the dance floor.

"Where were you two?" she said into his ear, not caring that people stared, not caring that they thought they knew her words.

"She showed up here, then we went to my place to practice for *American Prodigy*."

Courtney sighed. She knew about that dream. And her mom had mentioned guitar lessons for Ruby. Just not who would be giving them.

"She said she had permission. Anyway, she's a lovely girl, Court. You did a really good job."

Courtney laid her head on Edward's shoulder. If she just lived in this moment forever, everything would be okay.

But then the song was over, and the stage was her daughter's and Edward's. He must have been playing regularly because he sounded flawless and so did Ruby. They harmonized on a song she didn't know as if they'd been singing together for a lifetime. The crowd roared. The Angry Angels looked impressed with Ruby.

After the song, some kind of spell was broken. Ruby was tired and wanted to go home. Too many people and too many shallow conversations made Courtney want the same. Edward was distracted with his band and his bar and his friends. Mother and daughter slipped away undetected.

On the ride home, Courtney was silent until Ruby said, "He loves you, Mom."

"Now, honey, stop that. There's a lot you don't know."

"So tell me."

"I will. Just not tonight."

Chapter Five

Courtney thought she'd see Edward Saturday before the reunion, and maybe they'd talk or spend some time together, but that didn't happen. She didn't hear from him. He needed space. She had to give it to him even though it was the hardest thing she'd ever done. What was wrong with her?

She lay in a hammock in her mother's back yard reading a book of poetry and let it fall on the grass when she read the final line, "I have wasted my life." Had she wasted her life? The one she should have lived with Edward? Had he realized it already, and they could never get it back?

A woman can never say, when she has a child, that's ever a wrong turn or a waste. Children are gifts. Life's most precious.

Still, if she stayed, he'd have to pay attention to her.

The mystery was why she'd waited so long. Just stubborn maybe, waiting for him to come to her. And he never did. So they were both stubborn. Or just living their lives. Their other, parallel lives. It seemed incredible to her now that there was ever a time when she forgot about him, expected to live out her entire life never seeing him again, never touching him again. But now, she'd been given this opportunity, and maybe it was the time to put things right. She felt it. Even though everything was all wrong and the timing could not be worse, she believed in Edward. In the two of them.

So where was he? The fact that he obviously adored Ruby should show him he could love the baby too. She knew she expected a lot from people. From Edward. From Xander. She expected Xander to walk away from a life he'd carefully planned. She expected Edward to step right in. Edward. He was all she thought about. What was he doing right now? Busy at his bar, maybe. But not one little text? He might be enjoying tormenting her.

He might be playing her, paying her back, then when she said yes, when she told Xander all was over, when she announced to her family she and Edward were still married and were giving it another shot, only then he'd say, "Kidding, bitch."

He had a right. Well, maybe not a right as a decent human being, but she wouldn't blame him for wanting revenge. Hardly anybody was a decent human being all the time. She wasn't. Look at her now, ready to leave Xander, leaving him, taking their baby. She had thought about telling him she'd miscarried. This early in the pregnancy, it happened all the time. But he'd demand tests. Could she abort? She didn't think so.

She was so confused. She should go over to the house and pitch in on the cleaning, although her folks were so elated she was moving back to Blue Lake they'd hired a team of professionals to clean and handle minor repairs on her new home and probably she'd just be in the way.

Her phone rang and her heart popped. Edward?

"Is this Doctor Fass?"

"Yes," she answered automatically.

"Hi, I ah, I hear you have a new practice here in Lakeland County, and I wondered if I could make an appointment."

"I am setting up shop in Blue Lake, but things aren't quite ready. Maybe call back in a few weeks?"

"But, but…" The woman began to cry. "Can we just talk? I went to school with you. Sharon Patterson."

"Oh, Sharon, hi." She didn't think Sharon had been at the bar last night. But maybe. Early. Yes. And then she'd left in tears. Without her husband, who seemed totally unconcerned.

"Can we meet for coffee or something? Off the record? And then maybe I'll need you. I think I do. It's hard right now. Please say yes. I'm desperate."

Courtney invited her over. Just old friends (they never really were) having coffee and talking. Mom made coffee and set out a plate of cookies. She offered the back porch. Courtney thought about high school and last night and her social anxiety. People thought she was stuck up, thought herself too good for the town, but that wasn't it. She was just better one on one or in a creative collaboration. Those were the areas where she shined. So this would be fine.

Sharon was a mess when she came screeching around the corner in her sports car.

Her mascara was running down her cheeks, and her eyes were bloodshot. She looked like she hadn't slept in a week.

After they both sat, Courtney in a chair facing Sharon on the sofa, Courtney said, "You didn't stay long at Eddie's last night. Did something happen?"

"No. Yes." Sharon cried quietly into a tissue. "I couldn't face people. I feel like such an ass. Like everyone knows but me."

Courtney's mom had supplied a box of tissue which Courtney nudged in Sharon's direction. The one she held to her face was in tatters.

Sharon grabbed a fresh tissue and blew her nose with alacrity. Like she'd decided something. Still, she didn't talk. Courtney tried again. "This is just between us, as friends. I'm not saying anything to anyone. Tell me in as few words as you can if the whole story is too difficult."

"He, my husband, I saw him put his hands on another man's ass last night. I wasn't drinking. I didn't imagine it. He was loaded, so I was driving. Plus we have three kids. I needed to be sober to deal with the babysitter and my littlest is just two." Now that she'd started, the story poured out. "We've been married ten years. We have a great sex life. He's a little crabby sometimes, and he does lots of stuff with his buddies, but…" More sobs.

"Okay. That is a tough one. Did you talk to him about it?"

"No! I couldn't believe what I was seeing. I'm thinking I might be nuts. It can't be real. There has to be an explanation."

"You should ask him for one."

"I'm afraid."

Courtney didn't ask what Sharon was afraid of. She knew. Sharon was afraid it was true. Sharon was afraid her love was a lie. Sharon was afraid her life had been wasted. Sharon saw change everywhere and no way out, and she was scared. Courtney knew this because she felt the same way. Some therapist.

****

Courtney sat on the vanity chair applying mascara. Her third coat. She thought about Sharon and wished her well, but she saw the future one of two ways. Sharon accepted her husband as he was, or she got out and started over. Ruby came in, distracting her in a good way. She went straight to the closet they were sharing, opened it, and stared.

Courtney took a final look, decided she had not overdone it, and turned off her makeup light. She was here, she was staying, she was fighting for Edward. There was still the little problem of telling Xander, but she'd do that, too. Concerned, understanding Xander. He'd given her her second career. He knew she was afraid to drive in the rain. Just another quirky phobia that had popped up during the college years. But Xander counseled her and even prescribed her medication. He ignored her bad habits, like martinis and that lethal third glass of wine—well, at least she wasn't doing that anymore. Thank you, baby. She absently patted her tummy.

It had been a long time since she'd lived with Edward. She'd been fearless then. He wouldn't know this new, anxious Courtney. Would he be able to handle her? And what about him? What if he had stuff she couldn't deal with? The other women? Would they be appearing regularly, trying to win him back? Why wouldn't they? She was.

She looked into the full-length mirror at her face, full of artifice. Shrugged. So she was painted. It gave her confidence. Everyone else would be prettied up tonight, too. She put on a paisley mini dress and zipped a boot as Ruby chose an outfit and laid it out on her twin bed.

"What are you doing tonight, honey?"

"Moooo-oom. I tried to tell you. I got that job."

This was the first Courtney had heard of a job.

Ruby gave an exaggerated sigh. "There's this job. I saw it at the grocery story in town on a board. I'm going to be the videographer's assistant."

"At the reunion?"

"Duh."

Courtney ignored the remark. Fourteen was the year of snark. Ruby had been around video shoots her entire life until they'd moved on. She'd never shown the slightest interest in the business. She played guitar. She wrote bad poetry and translated it to the same three chords on her guitar into song lyrics. Courtney knew that in her mind, this made Ruby feel closer to Edward and was a defense against Xander, who Ruby saw as an interloper. Which, technically, he was. God, how had Courtney never seen that before? Had there ever been a day when she'd said, "Move in"? Had there ever been a night when she'd said, "Stay"? She didn't think so.

"What time does this gig end?" Courtney had planned to leave early. Another night of socializing on such a big scale just might drive her crazy.

"Don't worry. Lily said she'd drive me home. You can leave early like you always do." Ruby knew all about Courtney's aversion to large groups of people. She'd even seen a panic attack or two, which is how Xander convinced Courtney to try Xanax. At least she could drive in the rain with a tiny dose of the pill should there be an emergency.

Courtney would not be leaving Ruby out alone. It was time to face her social fears and get over them already. Look at it like a job. She'd never had anxiety meeting rock stars and dealing with their entourages. Why should this be any different? Well, then the focus was on the rock stars, not her. And she'd been in creative collaboration mode. She did not need pills to conquer her fears. She just needed to accept that she was human and flawed like everyone else.

Ruby had a bit of an obsession with Edward, but that was his problem now. If it became something neurotic, Courtney would deal with it. But Edward seemed to like Ruby just fine. Of course, he didn't know about the turkey baster. How Ruby had been convinced that Courtney had captured Edward's sperm, frozen it, kept it frozen for years, and then inseminated herself with Ruby, Edward's child. It was a silly little girl's dream, and it broke Courtney's heart. Ruby had finally let that go once Courtney broke down and showed her the paperwork from the sperm bank.

Ruby threw on a pair of jeans that looked exactly like the ones she discarded in a heap on the floor. She pulled an orange T-shirt over her straight dark hair. Edward's hair. She laced up sturdy work boots, as if a simple reunion video shoot (did they still call them video shoots or was it now a digital recording?) required set-level care.

Ruby had recently just started wearing a little bit of makeup and when Courtney thought of her own smudged mascara and kohl at that age, her red lips and bleached blonde hair with two inches of dark roots, she thanked stars for her sensible Ruby.

They were silent during the rest of their prep. Courtney's hair took full concentration. Ruby's glossy long and thick strands needed one hundred brush strokes. Slow, methodical. Courtney's hair was dark blonde these days, chin length, with no roots. They both sprayed clouds of hair product, then perfume, then chose earrings, hoops for Ruby and pearl studs for Courtney.

"Have fun, dears," her mom said as they came down the stairs. Dad grunted his approval.

They arrived at Blue Heaven just as the sun set into the water. The gazebo was strung with lights, their school colors, blue and green.

And Ruby spied a young girl, Lily, the one Courtney had talked to about rape and murder, connection not made until now, but of course it would be this troubled girl Ruby would seek out. Courtney gave herself an internal shake. Ruby would be fine.

****

Lily leaned against the Jeepster with her favorite camera casually wrapped around her neck, waiting for Ruby to leave her mom. She'd taken a few candids before darkness started creeping in, external shots, a few short video bursts she could splice into the movie. Every couple got their moment of arrival, but no fancy fake background. They could stand in front of the gazebo if they demanded atmosphere. Most of them just smiled, giddy, back in time. Lily could not imagine ever being that old. She felt ancient at twenty-five. To be forty? She didn't know if she'd make it.

She unconsciously rubbed her special gun pocket. Happiness is a warm gun, she thought, touching the cloth that covered it. She never cared that it stuck out a little bit. People assumed it was a camera lens.

Every minute or two she took a still. But when Ruby finally detached from Courtney, she immediately began instructing Ruby in setup as they went inside.

There were tripods and straps and boxes in the front office that needed taking upstairs to the party room. And she still had to take photos of the new arrivals. Ruby quickly and efficiently took all the larger equipment up the stairs, making several trips.

Lily was waiting for Eddie. She wanted to ask him about her idea, or at least tell him the story, up to and including Bob's theory of what could have happened to her mother. She wouldn't ask him to help her get a taped confession, but she'd say she wanted to do it, and get his reaction. Once Bob had let slip that Eddie's best friend was the police chief, that clinched it. She had to speak to him. Tonight. She wasn't sure if her plan broke any laws, although Dean had said, "Several," when she'd told him. Then he'd said, "Don't." Man of few words, Dean. Eddie was like that, too.

All this whirled through her brain while she snapped stills people would put in frames and hang over their mantels. That was her bread and butter. The movie, well, she'd see how many people were willing to pay fifty bucks for a long night of nothing but depressingly old people. Well, and Eddie and Courtney, the stars. She could make it a story about them with the other couples getting their face time. Where was he?

The reunion committee came out to greet Courtney as if they had not seen each other last night, so Lily filmed that. Ruby was old news, at least. People said hi to her, but the renewed buzz about her being Edward's child, even after their song at the bar, was not being talked about, at least that Lily could hear and capture on tape. This was all really good practice for her actual Big Event. Capturing vocals on tape was trickier than you'd think.

Courtney said hi to the women, looking around as the committee moved *en masse* to greet others. She waved Lily off, so Lily stopped taping her and panned to a beer tent set up next to the gazebo. Eddie wasn't working it. A server offered red or white wine on a silver tray and Courtney briefly walked into her shot, choosing water. Interesting. Lily panned to Courtney's flat tummy, then zoomed back to her face. She looked at least ten years younger than most of the frizzled, frazzled, dumpy women who made up the majority of the class of '92.

"Looking for Eddie?" Lily heard someone ask Courtney. She moved in. The speaker on this camera was very good, but only if you were close enough.

Courtney didn't respond to the classmate. Instead she walked inside Blue Heaven, the resort where the party was being held and coincidentally, the place where Lily was staying while in town. She'd had plenty of time to film the interior shots so took a moment to go over the guest list with Ruby.

"See, these check marks are for the people who have had their pictures taken. We need to find these folks, snap a pic, then check them off the list. Preferably before they are shit-faced." Some people were still arriving. Eddie had not gotten here yet, so Lily wasn't worried about missing any taping of the big meeting between the old sweethearts. She wondered if she should talk to Eddie before or after the party. After. Or she'd play it by ear. See how things unspooled.

Finally Eddie arrived and made a big deal of Ruby. Lily wasn't sure if she should film it, but as Ruby was part of the Eddie and Courtney story, she ended up doing a quick sequence until Eddie nodded at her and walked inside. Lily followed. Ruby tagged along.

Lily let Eddie get halfway up the stairs to the party room before she followed. "I'm going to be taping your mom and Eddie a lot. They're the big news of this reunion."

"I know."

"So, people will want to buy the video if they know they might see some kind of scoop." Then Lily rushed up the staircase to catch the big meet between old lovers. "Is it true they were married?" She whispered this to Lily, flipping on the sound to the video camera so it would get her voice. Ruby shrugged. Lily sighed. Just like last night, the speakers in the room played songs from 1992.

"This is their song," Ruby said.

Lily turned on the camera, listening. "Not your traditional love ballad," she said to Ruby.

"He wrote and recorded it for her." Ruby said it clearly enough that Lily knew she'd caught the words. Gold. Then she got the image. Eddie leaning into Courtney, whispering something into her ear, as the song he wrote for her played in the background.

Lily kept her camera trained on the couple. Nobody noticed because their eyes were on Eddie and Courtney, too.

Courtney gave her head a little shake but turned it into a hair toss. It was almost a foregone conclusion. They were together again. Eddie had come around to face her and they embraced and kissed like old friends might.

Lily told Ruby to hold the backlight higher. "Line it up with my camera angle."

Courtney said something, then smiled at Eddie.

The room was abuzz. Lily wasn't going to get any dialogue this way. She edged closer to the couple in time to hear Eddie say "Yeah, we could cause a real ruckus if you want."

People around them began to dance, trying to get in the frame. Lily was used to that. It was fine. Eddie and Courtney had realized they were standing in the middle of the dance floor. They moved. So did Lily and Ruby. Lily tracked as the couple of the hour headed to a wall with a pair of long sofas against it.

Lily stayed at a discreet distance while Courtney sank into the sofa, Edward plopping down next to her. A crowd gathered around them, which made edging in a little easier for Lily. People grabbed foot stools, floor, the other seats on the sofas. Eddie inched closer to Courtney so someone else could sit down. He put his hand on her knee. Her naked knee. Lily caught it on film. Everyone gawked, but Courtney just let out a laugh and let his hand stay where it was, the only uncovered part of her body. He took her hand in his and would not let go. He tugged lightly, and they rose together.

Eddie looked at the assembled crowd, kept his gaze a moment longer on Lily, and said, "Be right back." Then he pulled Courtney along after him. He stole her away, down the stairs, outside and probably, if Lily had to guess, around to a big front porch. She pretended to film the party for two or three seconds. Then she handed Ruby a point and click and told her get some candids of the dancers. "Be right back," she said, following Eddie and Courtney at a discreet distance.

Lily's quarters were below the banquet room, next to the resort office. Nobody had a key but her. She let herself in quietly and saw shadows on the big porch that faced the lake. Her porch.

"The place has changed since we came here back in the day." Lily picked up the voices.

"Yeah." Lily heard Courtney whisper, wasn't sure the camera caught it, but that was fine because she got to the window in time to see Eddie pull Courtney into his arms and kiss her. She didn't film it, but she must have made a noise.

The couple pulled apart, realizing Lily had found them. Lily gave up and turned on the porch light. "Sorry. I promise that did not go in the movie. These are my quarters. I just came down for a piece of equipment."

"Uh huh," Eddie said, clearly not believing her. "We appreciate that. Now we've got to go. Can you get Ruby home after the job?"

"I'll come back for her. Eleven o'clock," Courtney insisted.

And that was that. She didn't get to ask Eddie about the plan, nothing. Damn. Well, she'd just go to the bar for breakfast tomorrow. Hmmm. She could bring Bob. Between the three of them, she should be able to put together a more solid plan than "get confession while pointing gun." Like when, where, how, and who was going to help her.

She trudged up to film the end of the party. Daniel had trusted her to do a job, and she would do it right. Damn, sometimes doing the right thing sucked.

****

Desire drummed an uneven pulse at the back of her throat as Courtney hopped into the cab of Eddie's truck. He turned the key as longing tapped out a loud beat.

83

They drove the road to the river. Want burned into need, burned itself like a brand into her heart. I need you, Edward. Forget tattoos on skin, these words were engraved by fire on her soul. Their world of two, when they made it to the river, brimmed with luminous promise.

Once inside the glass house, Courtney placed herself inside Edward's careful kiss. Yes, she silently said. I want this. They hadn't spoken a word since leaving the reunion, but then, no words were necessary. Their bodies told the story with every step up the staircase. This was not attraction, this was adoration. She remembered the countless cherished moments of their past and allowed her true love to slip her dress from her shoulders.

The island of privacy Edward's loft afforded made her feel like she used to feel. Safe. Cared for. Protected. She hadn't realized before this moment that an area of this glass house was plastered and painted like a shrine to deeply private love. Edward's mouth grazed her shoulders, easing her dress and his lips lower. Finally, as her dress fluttered to the floor, she braved a peek into his eyes. There she saw a promise of sweet connection. This was something they'd known before, now studded with fresh treasure. That greedy need for skin on skin set her head spinning, her heart thumping. As his hands ran over her body, her mind melted into a blank slate of wonderful.

His mouth imprinted heat as he took sexy pleasure in her neck, her lips, her breasts. She arched her back, pressed against him. By some magic he'd got them both naked even while she had clung so fiercely to him. He swept her up and into his arms, and for a moment she was suspended in primal air. She forgot to breath until he settled her on his bed. This connection went soul deep. She was never more sure of anything in her life.

He floated above her, a luminous presence. His caresses continued, hands leading mouth, leaving a glowing trail of grace. His actions spoke more than a million words and she returned every gesture with one of her own. He let out a low sound when she curled her hand around him, slowly parting her fingers into a V and taking her fingers to the root of him. In joyful harmony, their bellies built fires. As fires do, one leapt to the next, connecting them through elements as old as time.

She knew this dance, had never forgotten the deeply treasured steps. Then he reached across her belly and opened a drawer at the bedside. She heard a crinkle and took the foil from his hand. Grinning like a pirate, she tore open the condom with her teeth. She smoothed the casing over him, then guided him inside. A moan of satisfaction escaped her. He was hers now. As proof, the gleam and slick essence led them from slow, measured motion into impossible unstoppable urgency. She opened her knees wide to greet Edward exploding inside her.

Edward collapsed on top of her; thoughts began to wander in. Let them come. She had nothing to hide, nothing to fear. She had only to look at the truth, straight on. It had never been like this with anyone else. Ever. How had she forgotten? It didn't matter. All that mattered was he keep kissing her. Everywhere. That's when she realized he'd started again and also the moment all thought once again fled.

Edward let out a rumble that sounded like triumph.

He looked down at her and laughed. She laughed back, yes, it was real, truly them, together again. Funny how time caught up with them. How it wound around them until they snapped into an easeful encore. They'd caught and held fast their particular rhythm after all this time apart. And this time, she'd do whatever it took. She'd never let him go. Not ever again.

Again her man draped himself over her as random thoughts of what time it was, where she had to be soon, drifted across the sky of her mind. Then Edward rubbed his stubbled jaw across her cheek and she shivered. Edward, I still love you, she said, but only in her head. He noticed her shiver and lifted himself off her, standing next to the bed, tucking her into a soft blanket.

"Warmer now?"

Edward's blood ran hot. It always had. He slept with windows open in the winter, and this was northern Michigan. Despite the blanket, she felt a chill. She didn't want to admit—not yet—that this would be no easy dream, no smooth coming together again. Yet he was her husband. She had never stopped loving him. She was at this moment in love with him. In her body, in her head, it was all Edward. Couldn't he see? Didn't he know? She yearned for him to say he loved her, too. "I've missed you without knowing it all these years." The realization that this time she had said the words aloud broke over her.

He stayed silent. Turned away.

Is it possible he doesn't love me the same way? Stuff had happened in the intervening years. He was able to flirt, get her into his bed, emotionally engage her, wow her with unabashed awesome sex, but perhaps true intimacy was no longer in his repertoire. She'd met guys like that in L.A. Hell, in L.A. every guy was like that. She let the silence stretch until she felt uncomfortable. "Why did you bring me here?"

He didn't answer, and her chill grew more pronounced.

Was this whole night, this entire weekend, an elaborate ruse just to get back at her for running out on him? Or was there another reason? Or was she being silly? Was everything just fine? Where her mind had been on vacation while they made love, now it raced in ten directions at once.

"For this, silly." He turned for one brief moment and kissed her on the forehead, then disappeared into the closed off area of the loft. She heard water running. Ah, the shower. Washing her off. Fine. She'd lay in his bed and figure this out, and then she'd go pick up Ruby. She and Edward might be okay, or they might have their break up all over again. Was she panicking for no reason? The problem for her was that she couldn't do without him now. Even if that's all it was for him, a bit of fun, a trip down memory lane sans clothing, she couldn't raise any anger. If he had been playing her, maybe she deserved it. She'd left. She'd hurt him. She was also cheating on Xander. For the first time, she felt shame wash over her and hook into her heart.

Edward and the pregnancy. He had pretended not to care, but maybe he did. As he took the longest shower in history, she made up story after story about why they couldn't just go back to how good things had been. They had eighteen years to clean up. Messy ones. That was why. Her pregnancy was unexpected but not unwanted. Still, at her age, searching for the happy family myth. She saw plenty of evidence of happy families here in Blue Lake. Her feelings tore back and forth, California, her clients in whom she'd invested so much, in whom she hoped for so much, and then herself, here, and what she wanted for her baby. For Ruby. It was not Xander.

Would Xander fight for parental rights? She didn't think so. His attachment to his wife was still too strong, as much as he denied it. He said he wanted to marry her, but she knew the deep ambivalence within him. He had been her mentor, and she had surpassed him in income long ago. Now he lived to support a wife he did not love and keep a house he did not live in.

Xander could not afford another child. He could not afford her. But if they married, he would have access to her wealth. Her parents had money as well. All around, this was a sweet deal for Xander. Except—maybe he still loved his wife. He'd never once acted like she was a pain, a problem. Well then, let him go back to her. Let Courtney raise her baby alone, as she'd raised Ruby.

As much as she hated it, she realized she was justifying what she and Edward had just done. Was it wrong? Where was the book that would tell her if cheating on her lover with her husband was morally repugnant? Okay, there wasn't such a book. Probably not even a blog. But what about ethics? Her own sense of ethics reminded her that she should have broken off one relationship before she took up another. That was the truth, and she had ignored it.

A Beatles song drifted out from the closed off section of the loft. An old song about love. If she loved Xander, she would not hesitate to share everything she owned. But she *had* shared. For years now. Waiting for him to divorce, waiting to be a real family. And they'd never even talked about it until she'd been late, bought a test, found out she was pregnant. That changed everything. Somehow, Xander had been revitalized. He had begun to make immediate plans. He had taken her ring size and kissed her belly. He ignored his wife's calls more often than not. And he asked her to divorce Edward and marry him.

She sighed. She'd been carried away too. Her life's dream, in front of her for the taking. She took it. And now she wanted to thrust it back and revise that old and shopworn dream. She could dream a better dream now. Here. Instead of helping rich women find their bliss, she could help addicts find their sobriety. Help women accept or let go of their sexually ambivalent husbands. She could help troubled teenagers and young adults find a better path after abuse and violence at home or school. And she'd make herself a better path too. With or without Edward.

Someone banged on the glass door. She slipped on Edward's black T-shirt. It came almost to her knees. She sat up as he came out of the sanctuary.

"Someone's at your door."

"I hear."

"May I use your shower?"

Edward took in her garment with one long look up and down her body. "Sure."

Then they both heard the voice yelling her name.

Edward opened a drawer and handed her a pair of clean boxers. "It's him, isn't it?"

Xander.

"I'm not going down there without you."

So she put on the ludicrously baggy boxers and

followed Edward down the stairs, holding the elastic around the waist so her pants would not fall on the ground, trip her, and launch her in a dramatic fall down the stairs. She curled into a corner of the sofa as Edward opened the door.

Xander walked in. "Don't you believe in doorbells?"

Edward sat down right next to her. Xander paced. In her mind, she was in bed with Edward the way it should have been. She had one hand on his heart. She loved his chest, bare and bronze. Xander's voice, his gray tufts of chest hair escaping from his golf shirt, interfered with her lovely daydream.

"What the hell is going on, Courtney? A final fling?" Funny what he chose to say first. Funny how the situation inside the house with no bell was second on his mind. He seemed more agitated than angry.

"I don't have a bell because I don't entertain guests. Until you all came to town."

For some reason this sparked Xander's anger. Edward's tone, his lack of apology or embarrassment. Courtney's stomach pitched as if she really were falling down the stairs.

****

Eddie didn't like it, not any of it. Yes, he loved Courtney in some crazy complicated way, but this was his house for one, and it had felt overly populated ever since she'd come to town.

"Let's settle things right now. The three of us." Xander. Voice of reason. Big shot professor.

Eddie didn't offer anyone a drink. He was done being the polite host. He did not want this guy here. But Courtney was here, and she was reaching for his hand.

He took it and sat next to her, tucking her hand into his lap. "She's my wife." She didn't feel like his wife, but he felt her need of him, and he could not deny her. He had never been able to do that. What kind of a name was Xander anyway? What was wrong with Alex?

Xander tried to embrace Courtney, to lift her off the sofa and away from Eddie but the two held firm. Eddie felt a moment's hot shame. He'd gone after Courtney and then when he'd found out about the baby he'd balked. Just like before. He put his other hand on top of hers. Enclosing her hand in both of his. Sending her messages he didn't quite understand.

Xander stood in the middle of the big room, hands at his sides. Suddenly he dropped to one knee, in front of Courtney, and took a ring box from his pocket. "I love you, Courtney. I don't deserve you. But would you please do me the honor of being my wife?"

"Don't you have one of those? A wife? Because this one's mine." Eddie couldn't resist. And he did not release Courtney's hand. Unfortunately it was not the hand an engagement ring traditionally appeared on. Before a stunned-looking Courtney could answer, Xander had grabbed her other hand and shoved the ring on her finger. Perfect fit. Huge stone. Not the kind of ring people around here wore, no matter how much money they had. Sucker was the size of a quarter.

Courtney looked into Eddie's eyes, hers filled with panic. Then she slowly took her hand away from his. She slid the ring off her finger and tucked it back into the box Xander still held. "No, dear. I'm sorry."

Eddie breathed relief.

"Does he—" Xander spat. "Know about the baby?"

"Yes. Yes, I do." He felt Court snake an arm

around his, entwining them.

Xander awkwardly rose to his feet.

"I'm not coming home, Xander. I'm staying here."

"But I cut my golf weekend short to do this thing." He lifted the ring box that clung limp in his hand.

"I'm so sorry."

"Our baby."

"There is no baby."

This was a surprise to Eddie. Courtney had never been able to lie convincingly but Xander seemed to believe her despite the fact that she was biting her bottom lip and her foot was beating time like a metronome.

"What?"

"Spontaneous abortion. Happens all the time." She shrugged, and real tears fell from her eyes. What the hell? Had she really lost the baby?

****

Sunday morning, Eddie drove to the bar early. He had a stop to make before doing the breakfast thing for the tourists. Best damn Bloody Marys in town, mimosas for the dainty ladies, as well as bacon, sausage, eggs, hash browns, and toast. Rye or sourdough, those were the choices. He baked sausage and bacon in the oven, did up an industrial pan of scrambled eggs, and used shredded raw potatoes prepped by staff the day before, which he spread out on the oiled grill to let them crisp. Still, there was a lot to do to get that mess plated, and he was glad of it.

Courtney had not lost the baby. She had lied. And accused Xander of giving her his wife's ring. Xander didn't deny it. He took the ring and left. That's when she told Eddie she'd lied to Xander about the baby, because yes, there was still a baby, but she needed to "get him off her back." Eddie had been paralyzed with a kind of horror. Who was this woman and where was his Courtney? She had looked at her phone, then at him, said, "Sorry, babe, I gotta pick up Ruby." Then she changed from his clothes to her dress and left. No explanation, no remorse, nothing.

He knocked at her door, and she opened it still in her robe. Her folks, he knew, were at church. He handed her the envelope with his signature on the divorce filing. Then he said good-bye. So he drove away again, ending after ending with this woman, his wife, at least for now. It was good he had eggs to crack and whisk and stir. Because he needed to be busy and not to think about this woman any more. She and Xander deserved each other.

Before he'd even gotten everything prepped, in popped Bob and Lily. Eddie eyed the videographer warily. She might be as crazy as Courtney. You just never knew with women. The way she'd followed them around like she was making a documentary of their lives or something. It was way off base. She didn't have her camera with her this morning, but when she swung her purse onto the bar, it made a distinctive thwack. Like a gun. He eyed the little suede fringy thing. It was just big enough for a lady gun and a driver's license.

Christ. Lily and Bob didn't watch where they walked at all, they only watched each other. Funny how Lily was a videographer; she should be a model with those cut cheekbones, full lips, and jutting hips. Her blonde hair hung shiny and long and was just dark enough to look natural. She was a beauty, and her adoration of young Bryman was apparent. Also apparent, the feeling was entirely mutual and so thick he could smell it. This made him feel unsettled.

Had he ever been that young? He'd been that in love. Once. But Courtney had changed. He didn't want to think about her. His eyes went to the fringed suede purse casually slung across his bar. Other folks had started trickling in. Just a few but still. He had one waitress on and she poured a pitcher for his geezer regulars at the far end of the bar, then went over to the two full tables by the dance floor. What would Lily need with a gun? And did he really want it on his bar?

Lily and Bob finally quit staring in adoration at each other long enough to acknowledge his presence. He set cardboard coasters in front of them. "What'll it be?"

"Two breakfasts, eggs scrambled, and two Virgin Marys."

That's how good his mix was. People ordered them without the vodka all the time. Especially early in the day. He poured out drinks and went into the kitchen, popped toast into the six slicer, sipped strong coffee only he was drinking.

After he served the love birds, he went to the end of the bar to shoot the breeze with his geezers. Nothing new there. Just like everyone else in town, they wanted the dirt on Courtney.

"Ancient history." Eddie didn't want to discuss Courtney. Not now, not ever.

"Oh, yeah, that, you used to go out with her a hundred years ago."

"And we been hearing youse are keeping company again."

Keeping company. Such a quaint phrase for what

they'd done last time they'd been together. Was it just last night?

One of the geezers had been their science teacher in high school. Thank god he had not been at the reunion, although a few of the teachers had shown. He hadn't seen Eddie sneak Courtney away before the party really got started. Of course it would be on the video for everyone to see if Ms. Lily had her way. He'd have to talk to that young lady about editing. And guns in bars.

"So, Eddie." Geezer Teacher laughed, his back teeth empty sockets. "We heard she bought Doc's place. She's back. We got us an honest to pete head-shrinker in town now." He shook his head in wonder.

"I heard about that," Eddie said. He pretended urgent business at the other end of the bar, but the lovebirds whispered intently to each other. They didn't need a thing. He went into the kitchen, buttered their toast, plated up their order and refilled his coffee mug. Black. Like his mood.

Well, damn it, he was sorry, he just couldn't do it. Go back. Try again. The whole foundation of the thing was shaky. It was made of air. All that distance. All the years. They could never be together the way she wanted to; he could never raise another man's kid as his own knowing the true father had no clue he had a child in the world. Like Ruby's dad. Four hundred kids, Ruby had told him. He didn't give a damn about having a kid in the world, that guy. But the guy with the diamond ring the size of a quarter that he'd maybe stolen from the finger of his current wife, he cared.

It was too much for Eddie. It wasn't enough. He had too much to lose. Not material things but integrity.

He'd built himself into someone who, admittedly, was a little loose with the ladies, he was human, but otherwise a solid citizen and pillar of the community. He remembered the days and months after Courtney had left. His rage burned so hot. He scorched every woman he took to bed. He'd left burn marks. He'd scarred some. He was ashamed of his early behavior. He'd had to crawl out of that hole she'd dropped him into, and it had taken everything. His interest in cars. His interest in music. His interest in anything. He drank too much for a couple of months, then stopped that shit. It only made things worse. He bought the bar without thinking through why. He had to do something with his life. The previous owner died. The place, while not a gold mine, was a good earner. He had a little bit of money, and Daniel Bryman, the town benefactor, had loaned him the rest. Eddie paid him back early and with interest. Turned out summer people liked his idea of getting new bands in to play every night, and sometimes all day. It had been a no-brainer, and he'd been able to turn his mind off. Did the Zen thing. Ambled along observing life, partaking of a willing accomplice in bed, but with a softer attitude that still included a get of jail free card at the end of the night.

He was now the man he would be for the rest of his life. Things would settle down. This black mood would pass as easily as the coffee he'd just drunk without noticing. Emotion sucked. He liked the Buddhist idea: desire leads to suffering, so detach. Take desire out of the equation and maintain a nice serene existence. There could not be anything with Courtney, not what she wanted, which seemed to be the same thing she wanted before she left. Sure it felt good to be with her, but it was all based on a lie. A huge deception. He couldn't do it. Somehow, he'd become good. He brought the lovebirds their breakfast.

Then Lily pushed her plate aside and whispered a story to him that curled his hair. And that was saying something for a guy with Native American blood. She was even crazier than Courtney.

"So will you help us?" Lily asked him.

"Is that a gun in your purse?" He didn't bother to reply. He'd talk to Bob later. Somebody had to straighten the kid out.

"What?" She blushed. "Why?"

"It's illegal to carry a concealed weapon in an establishment that serves alcohol. Least that's the last I heard. And you know my buddy is the police chief, right?" He kept his tone low so the geezers and the influx of tourists couldn't hear him.

Lily pulled her purse onto her lap, and someone took the seat next to her.

"Eat and go. And also. No." Eddie stared hard at Lily, then turned to Bob. "I'll talk to you later."

Chapter Six

Courtney put the envelope in a drawer and took out her journal. She hardly used it these days, but she needed a technique she often used in therapy. She was going to write a letter to Eddie. She would never send it, but she'd say on the page what she knew she would never share with another living soul.

"I'm thinking about you, of course I am. I realize how I screwed up in so many ways...I regret some things I said and did in the past, but I don't regret that we reconnected. I fell too far too fast, and that wasn't smart. It wasn't like me either. I didn't know what was happening except I liked it. I want to apologize for anything in my behavior that was inappropriate (which is so many things). What I think now is I was really unhappy and starting to realize it and you made me fully realize it, just the idea of you. When you seemed so content with your bar and your bands and your house of glass, it just made me happy for you but sad to realize that was not how my life is or ever was since Xander came into it—but that doesn't give me the right to think I can come back to town and take up where we left off. Pregnant with another man's baby." She stopped writing for a minute. At least she had cleared that up with Edward. She picked up her pen again. "You have a good life, and you're content, mostly. Maybe you have roads left in your shoes and if so, I hope you let them take you where you want to go. I just wish I had not crushed our friendship along with the romance. The romance was doing my head in because I want you so much. The friendship, precious and forever. But only in my heart. Has to stay there as I can't reach out to you any more than I have already done. I've done all I can, and then some. I've crossed a line, I know I have. Just by a little bit, but that's too much for me. All I can say is you carried me away with your charm and your love and your sexy self. All of it was just irresistible. I've never been strong as far as being able to pass up something I want really really bad. And I wanted you really really bad. I could tell that you were easing away after I told you about the baby, and you were trying to get us to slow down, and I just would not take the hint. I didn't value my partner as I should—but there's more to that story than you need to know. It's for me to work out and not your problem. I think you knew that, too, and sensed I needed room to figure things out without your influence. That's how good and kind you are. You're in my heart, baby. You'll never leave it again. This is a small town, but I suppose it's possible I might not ever see you again, or hear your voice, or even read a note from you to me, but I am not sorry any of this happened except how I hurt you and disturbed your life. That I am sorry for. I think you're a strong person, and you'll be okay, and you'll find your footing and probably already have, but any moment of sadness, anger, or anything else negative that I brought into your life, I regret. The good stuff was good, and I'm grateful for it all. Please find me in the next life or the next world and we will try to make it work. Love you, blood, bones, and soul, sweetheart. You are the ONE. And I lost you twice. Or…will you return to me, my love?" She crossed out the last lines, mad at herself for hoping for things that just were not going to come true. She shoved the journal in the drawer with the divorce papers and threw on a pair of jeans. Her only pair of jeans. Pulled a T-shirt over her hair still stiff with spray from last night.

Her family were all at church. Courtney was alone in the house. She felt seventeen again. She had to get out of here. Damn lot of good writing had done her. Her heart felt like it was filling her chest cavity, or maybe she was having a heart attack or was it just panic? She did her breathing and tried to settle down. She stumbled over to the bed and sobbed. She'd do anything for a Xanax right now. But the baby. She had to protect the baby. And that meant working through her upset in the most healthy way. Drop the story. Whatever it was. Feel the feelings. Let them pass through. Edward didn't love her. Stab. They were not going to get a second chance. Stab. Stay with the pain, let it flow, then let it go. She had fled her life in search of another, but it hadn't turned out exactly as she'd hoped. Wait, that was story. Stop it. Just feel the hurt, breathe it in and out. Her ongoing research in the field of neuroscience and the newish fMRI imaging proved that this type of behavior modification indeed settled the amygdala more quickly. Let the pain be heard; it will move on soon enough.

She expected to have a dull ache for a while. That was normal. But she had to build some purpose into her life, some sense of happiness outside of Edward. Happiness did not depend on a man. She had told that to so many women. But now she knew that she had lied. Because her happiness depended on Edward. Stop the story, she told herself. Breathe. Feel. Let go.

But she couldn't. So she walked. She walked to her new house only three blocks from where her parents lived. The furniture would be arriving tomorrow. She amazed herself with the speed at which she had turned her life upside down, but everything had pointed her in this direction. *If it flows, go. If it blocks, stop.* One of her tidy aphorisms. So easy to say and the first part easy to do. The problem came with trying to stop. She had to stop loving Edward. It felt so dark now. The sun was out, shining, a perfect day for the reunion picnic, but she was skipping it. The dark was in her, and she had to live with it and let it pass in its own time. For the baby's sake.

It had been wrong to tell Xander his child was dead. Maybe she should get an abortion so that the lie would become the truth. Oh no, that made the stabbing in her heart stronger, like she was stabbing her womb. She had to tell Xander the truth. He had to know. Where was he staying? Surely not Blue Heaven. She stood in front of her house. She'd stupidly left the key at her parents' place. Stop calling yourself stupid. She had her phone. She texted him. Where are you? No answer. He must be in the air, flying home. She started to text him again, the truth this time. He'd see it when he landed. But she felt faint, like she needed to sit down, or better still, lie down. She went around to the backyard. The lawn had been neatly trimmed, and everything looked move in ready. Someone had placed a hammock under the big maple tree. It had to have been her mother. A surprise. She knew how Courtney loved the one in her folks' yard.

There was a blessing she could count, right there. So she said a thank-you to the universe and tried to feel gratitude. It was too hard. All she felt, still felt, was pain. Physical pain. Pain that made her double over with grief and sadness. She let herself fall.

****

Courtney woke up in the hospital two towns south of Blue Lake, her mom and Ruby on either side of the hospital bed. "What happened?" But she knew. She'd lost the baby. Their eyes told it all.

Ruby said, "Sorry, Mom."

Then her mom explained about the surgery. How she'd had to have an emergency hysterectomy as well.

Courtney couldn't reply. She held her living girl's hand, hoping Ruby would never know Courtney herself had killed that little embryo as surely as if she'd stabbed her stomach with a knife. Her lies. Her emotions. Her darkness. It had all pushed that precious almost-being into nothing.

"I found you at the house when you didn't meet us after church," her mom said, patting Courtney's shoulder, then capturing her cheek with her soft hand. "I just had a feeling."

"Edward signed the divorce papers."

"Ah." Her mom gave her hand one last squeeze, even though there was an IV needle poking out of it with tape holding it in place. She was so tired. She wanted to fall asleep and never wake up, but she knew that was her pain talking, trying to take her under. And under scared her. Under like in a coffin. Her heart clutched, then sped. Buried alive. Her heart rushed so fast she couldn't breathe. She pushed the bell on her bed. Kept pushing.

"Get the nurse!"

Ruby rushed into the corridor. Unfortunately, her daughter had seen Courtney in full blown panic mode before. Ruby came back with a doctor and shoved Courtney's bottle of Xanax at him. Ruby must have gotten it from the medicine cabinet at Mom's. Bless that child.

"Panic disorder?"

Courtney nodded, barely hanging on. As far as phobias, this was a new one for her, but the panic washed over her the same way.

"I'll be right back." The doctor took her bottle of pills when he left. She had never wanted anything as much as she'd wanted that bottle of pills. A nurse came in an eternity later with two blue pills in a little paper cup. She handed the cup to Courtney and poured out a glass of water, but by the time she handed that over, Courtney had swallowed the pills dry, rocking herself and trying to breathe and being unable to or even explain to her terrified mom what was happening. "I'm going to die." Then, seeing Ruby's stricken face, she amended her statement. "I *feel* like I'm going to die." She had to be strong for her daughter. And her mother. She took the glass of water the nurse urged on her and sipped it.

"It's the panic," the efficient nurse told her mom and Ruby, giving Courtney a shot that instantly made her limp and relaxed. Where had the doctor gone? She floated down a dark, comfortable well. Peace. The nurse cleared the room. Courtney said goodbye to the people in the world who loved her the most. She watched them leave. It would be okay. Everything would be just fine.

She didn't sleep. Didn't want a sleeping pill on top of the shot and double dose of Xanax. It was safe; she was practically a pharmacologist she had referred so many patients. Feeling this peace was enough until the meds wore off sometime in the middle of the night. The duty nurse brought her another Xanax, but one only took the panic down to anxiety level. She could go through the anxiety now. She wasn't protecting anyone. Her mom would take care of Ruby. Her house would get put together. And somehow, one day, she would put herself back together again, too.

****

Lily was giddy. Bob was her best friend, and now he would be her lover. She'd wanted it, worked for it, tried to heal herself and be the woman he needed and deserved. She hardly touched her breakfast, although Bob devoured his.

"Keep your strength up, big fella. You're gonna need it."

"Huh?" Bob slammed down his empty glass with a bit more force than necessary. "You what?"

"I'm ready. I want to." Lily put this front on about being all confident and in control, but beneath that she was a scared girl, and she knew it. She'd never be ready. There'd never be a perfect time. But if she wanted Bob, and she did, she had to try. Maybe they'd fail, but she had to try. When was there ever a time in her life when she didn't at least do that?

Bob threw some bills on the bar, and they left for Blue Heaven. It was too bad Eddie wouldn't help them, but she could sense that Bob was in. He was considering it. All that was needed was for her to make love to him, bind herself to him. Then he'd do it. Lily had the bungalow to herself and she'd kept it sealed off from the outside; every blind closed tight, every curtain drawn, and every door locked. So even though the office was busy and a cleaning crew banged around upstairs, they had a cocoon of two.

She loved his sweet face. She did not deserve this devotion, but she was grateful for it. She went right into the bedroom and stripped. This is the way she'd done it before, but Bob seemed perplexed.

"Wait, wait," he said, kissing her neck and helping take off the final scraps of bra and panties, running his fingers over her body.

Then she was naked, and he was not. So she unzipped his jeans. Guys liked that. Right? They'd always seemed to. She prepared to go down on him with him standing right there still in his shoes because that was the fastest way and then they'd leave. Oh right, she thought, the goal here is penetration. Intimacy, not just sex. Not that penetration was intimacy exactly, but for her it was a trust thing. Still a hurdle after all these years. Her need for revenge burned like a hot coal when Bob touched her, his hands in her hair, pulling her up to face him.

Way more touching and kissing than she was used to. She unbuttoned his Sunday shirt. He was supposed to be at church but had picked her up and she talked him into going for breakfast instead. She'd had a sexy dream about him last night that surprised her. It woke her up at three a.m. It was a sign. Even before Eddie said no. Today was the day.

They lay naked under the sheets. Lily felt safe covered up at least in some way. Bob drew her nude body next to his, and she let him. He smoothed her hair away from her face. "I love you, Lily."

"I know. I love you." They kissed again, and she climbed on top of him. Guys liked that too. Whoa. She was lubricated. That didn't usually happen; usually it hurt.

She slid up and down him like he was a stripper pole. Guys liked that. She'd had a lot of practice, knew all their desires. She leaned down a little bit, brushing her nipples this close to his lips. He took the bait, but for her, it wasn't a win, she felt something too. Something like a string tugging her back to her dream last night and the sensations it had unleashed.

Bob put his arms around her waist and moved her below him, considerably slowing the pace she'd set. They looked right into each others' eyes and Lily liked what she saw reflected there. Reverence, joy, lust. This was going to be okay, she thought as she tumbled into the first orgasm of her life.

After, he held her with such tenderness that she cried.

"Oh honey, no, wait, was it—"

"Shhh. Not bad. Good. So good."

He stroked her arm and kissed her cheek. "It's okay now. You have me."

And my gun, Lily thought. Also cameras. Lots of cameras.

****

Tuesday, Courtney was released from the hospital, and her mom asked if she wanted help packing up her childhood bedroom. Courtney had decided it would be therapeutic to clean everything out. Throw it away. Give it away. Put it in her own attic. Courtney hadn't taken much when she'd moved out the first time, with

Eddie. Maybe clothes and makeup and that was it.

She had a checklist for the movers. The bedroom furniture. Her new house had three big bedrooms, and her mom had just gotten new mattresses. Wouldn't her mom want this stuff for a guest room herself? No, she would not. It was going to be a sewing room, a place to put photos (real ones, not digital) into albums, a place to quilt. It was going to be a craft space. Huh.

Edward's letter was in the back of the closet, under a pile of boxes filled with childhood mementos and keepsakes. She'd pulled out the boxes, intending to go through them one by one, when she found it, the lined school paper yellowed, the handwriting loopy and youthful, unlike Edward's mature scrawl on the divorce papers he'd handed her that morning, only a week ago, but that felt like years ago. The day she'd lost her baby.

"Dear Court, I love you honey with all my heart, blood, and bones. There isn't a piece of me that doesn't love a piece of you. I'm devastated right now, totally crushed by your words." What words? She couldn't remember. "The guys were goofing around, and we were drunk, and you did look damn hot in that dress. I am not going to apologize for that because it's true. My love for you is about more than your beauty, your soulful eyes, your brain teeming with ideas and schemes and thoughts that I can barely keep up with. My love for you—and I thought yours for me—is primal. It's at the bottom of everything. It invades my reptile brain and hijacks my neocortex. I'm a caveman when I'm with you. Those ancient genetics take over. You're mine. I'm yours. When you say we need a break, or we should date other people—" She said that? When? She never wanted anyone but him. She must have been pissed and paying him back. He acted like an ass with his friends sometimes. "I will give up the band. I will sell the car. I will never drink whiskey again. I do not need anyone but you. I prefer it that way."

A big slash and his name and then under than more words. "Whoa. Sorry. What just happened was I got thrown back by this giant tsunami of hurt. I was out of it, thinking about life without you. That can't happen. I won't let it. We can get past this thing and any other damn thing that comes. We have to because if we don't our lives will be shit. They will surely be fucked utterly…we need to be together now and always and I stand by those words. I'm bringing this letter to your house and putting it in your hand and if you tear it up after you read it I'll know it's true, you really do want to break up. But if something in my words touches you, like the fact that I will never love anyone but you, and I will always love you, so that means I will grow alone into a bitter old man, and you don't want that for me, now do you honey? I love you more than these words can express. Let me show you while your folks are at church. Come on. Let me into your Courtney places. We will be together always, my love. As I come to you with nothing except my bloody heart in my hands, my sincere apology on my lips, and the endlessly deep love in my eyes, take me in, I want to be lost in you. Your Edward."

Tears ran down Courtney's eyes. She'd cried so much these past few days. Were these new tears for Edward or the baby she'd lost? Some of what Edward had said came true. He never married. He was alone. He wasn't quite an old man, but soon. Why didn't he see now that they could change the trajectory of their lives, put it back in place, make the letter true again. She should show it to him. She moved it away so tear stains would not ruin it. The ink was faded enough on that most precious document.

Oh Edward. Oh little one. She sat among the detritus of her childhood, bruised and sore and beaten up. Why does youth squander happiness like there is a never-ending supply? Why had she thought she could possibly be happy or even fully alive without Edward? She had not been. She'd had moments. He'd had moments. They added to years of satisfaction perhaps, but nothing so intimate as this letter depicted. She would cherish it always.

Edward's way with words, the way he chose unusual ones, always searching for the perfect phrase to add to a song. That was in there. He had talent. He could do something with his life. She felt ashamed. Had she demanded he quit the band? He knew she didn't like the hot rods and the drinking combination. She worried, she said. She didn't want his pretty face to get smashed. His long muscular legs to break. His strong arms to snap. But the band. No. That was his life, his passion, and she knew what passion felt like. She supported it.

The phone rang. Edward. She clicked on without checking Caller ID. Xander. She was so shocked she didn't say anything.

"Are you there?"

"Yes."

"I got your text. Have you come to your senses yet? When will you be home?"

If it blocks, stop. Here's something she could stop. She had to stop. Now. Forever. "Xander. I bought a house. The baby is gone. I'm sorry." She really was, more than he could possibly know. At least now she was not lying. She held back a sob, then decided to let it out. He went on as if she were not crying. As if they had not just lost their child.

"It can be our summer place. The boys would love it. And I want to get to know your family."

She made no comment. That was the first she'd heard about him wanting any connection at all to her family.

"Xander. Go home and patch things up with your wife. It's been good, so let's end it on a good note."

"It has been good, that's what I mean."

Finally, she got him off the line, convinced him it was over. She'd tried to make them a family, working, cooking, cleaning, easing Ruby into a routine of acceptance of Xander, and sometimes, his sons. Ruby was a good girl and played along, but Courtney realized that that's all it was. Play. Ruby didn't care about Xander. And neither did she. She put her hand on her tummy, protective still of the child they'd made. Then she remembered as tears continued to fall.

She wanted to read the letter from Edward again. It made her forget the baby grief, at least for a few minutes. She read it again. Five times. Over and over like a love-sick teenager. She wondered where Edward was right now. She wondered what these pages would mean to him. To her, they called out across the years. They made her determined to win him back.

The movers came in and she put the letter in her purse, showing them which boxes to move to her new attic and which to leave on the back porch for the church.

Then she went to find her family at her new house.
****

Besides the few things she'd bought in Port Huron, the large foyer was beautifully decorated with a mirror and small settee. There were lamps and tables, upon which rested a bowl for keys and mail and family pictures in frames. "It's all stuff from the attic...of course you'll want to buy your own things, but this will get you started," her sister said. Though her mother, father, sister, brother, and Ruby all hovered, nobody mentioned the baby. But the house. If she could focus on the house. The house was glorious.

She'd had that one talk with Gwennie about color when they'd gone through shelter magazines. Her parents had gotten the house painted and waited for the furniture delivery yesterday, which she had totally forgotten about. Her beloved irritating awesome sister had faithfully reproduced the palette of pale moss green and deep rose red, not just on the freshly painted walls, but incorporating shades of the predominant colors into every room on the main floor.

The east side of the four square were the large foyer and stairway, then through to the kitchen. On the west side, the front parlor and the dining rooms weren't complete, she was glad of that. But as she walked through trailed by her loved ones, she saw that things were ready enough to live here.

In the kitchen, her dad and brother sat at the table, one she remembered from her grandmother's home before she'd retired to Florida. "Honey, I hope this is okay. You can change anything you don't like." The appliances Courtney had chosen, whimsical in their retro look but practical in their contemporary energy efficiency, had been yet another gift from her parents, who had done so much already.

"I'm overwhelmed," she said, meaning it. Even managing to smile. "Thank you." The place where her baby should be was raw and bloody. She deserved these stabs of pain. She'd brought them on herself. But Ruby, currently perusing a fully stocked fridge, deserved a whole mother, so she kept her pain in her pocket, like the letter in her purse.

She was in mourning, for the life that would never be, but also for Edward. Life was like that. Joys and sorrows. Both had to be experienced. Nobody got it all right. She wasn't sure what she'd done to turn Edward off so completely, but she was too tired to think about it now. He must have a reason, but she was confused and upset and not thinking straight, so what might otherwise be obvious just wasn't at the moment. Her grief was all mixed up into a heavy ball of pain she had to roll in front of her just to be able to move at all.

She looked out the back door. No hammock. Someone had taken it down. Likely the blood had ruined it. She wasn't sure she'd ever be able to lie in a hammock reading again. She suddenly hated all content smug people with lives that were like well-oiled machines, working away with ease and accord. Then she immediately felt guilty. She had a lovely daughter, a great family. They'd support her emotionally and even financially, although she didn't think she'd need her folks' money. It was Ruby she should be thinking of, not herself, not her own pain.

Ruby closed the fridge, said she'd already seen her room, approved everything. Could she go down to the beach, since it was a short walk and the day was fine, and it was time for her mom to have a pill and a nap?

Courtney felt utterly and completely exhausted. Her mother caught her in a hug as she swayed, almost faint. "We're just leaving. Ruby's right. You need to get your rest. I'm sure the beach is safe. Ruby's met lots of the kids, and she'll find someone to hang with, won't you dear?"

Courtney chuckled at her mother's use of slang, but she nodded and let herself be hugged and kissed. Gwennie and her mom stayed behind, helped her undress and get into her new bed. "Just for an hour," Courtney said, setting the alarm on her phone and putting it next to her bed.

Chapter Seven

Lily saw him across the street, pure chance. Through her lens, and not even the most powerful one. Her cousin was here, in Blue Lake. Stalking her. Now maybe Eddie would believe her. Reflex, honed over five years, compelled her to unzip her lens case, put away the equipment, and pull out her 9 mm gun. Tiny enough for her pocket, but accurate and lethal. The rosewood grip gave her a hit of instant relief. The hunter had no idea he was being hunted.

She tucked her gun and phone into her pockets and tracked him from a discreet corner of Sanchez's. Dinner time and the popular Mexican place hummed with tourists. She melted right in. He ambled along, not a care in the world. Pretty soon he'd care, by the time she was through. Her plan didn't include shooting the gun, although Dean, after years of training, had given her the ultimate compliment. He'd trust her to have his back. Not that such a situation would ever happen. But hypothetically. Dean's words meant everything to her. More than her degree, even. Way more.

All she wanted to do was point the gun at her cousin and tape his confession. Bob should be here to hold the camera while she held the gun, but things were moving too fast. If she didn't jump on this opportunity, she might never get the chance again to hear the whole of it. What he did to her at sixteen; what he did to her mom after Christmas. She had the best hollow point bullets money could buy, but she never intended to use them. She just wanted the best of everything. Something about training with Dean made her want to be that way. Prepared.

Damn. Her cousin had stopped to talk to a young girl. Ruby. Shit! They were laughing, and Ruby pointed to the bike shop on the edge of town. Then they turned and walked there together. No. That fucker had a baby face hiding his murderous heart, and Ruby looked a little older than fourteen. The town had grown so much in the past five years, even Lily couldn't tell tourists from townies. Ruby and that monster would be perceived as a casual summer hook-up. Nobody would blink.

Lily quickly threw her equipment into her trunk. Checked pockets. Phone. Gun. Good to go. She cut down the boardwalk and got to the bike shop just in time to see them come out. He grabbed a bike from the rack, and Ruby hopped on the handlebars. Fuck. They wheeled down the deserted bike path. She was well behind them. Even running, she soon lost visual.

Her mind tried to piece Ruby into the picture. Just a taunt. Because he could. She'd handed him Ruby on a pretty plate. She pulled out her phone, but who to call, what to say? She told Bob she was working, which wasn't a lie exactly, but would take too long to explain. Eddie didn't believe her, Courtney didn't know her, and Dean, the man she trusted like no other, was hours away. Also, nothing had happened. Yet.

When she heard Ruby scream, she yanked out her phone, pressed record, and shoved it back into her left pocket. A voice recording would have to do. This scenario was the one she had not prepared for, but she could handle it. She pulled her gun out of the specially stitched right pocket and slid off the safety in one smooth motion.

She walked, slow and steady, in the shadow of the giant pines along the path. Ruby was nowhere. There was no sound. Had that scream been laughter? A silly shriek? They had ridden the bike too far up the trail for Lily to see or hear. She was not taking chances. She held her gun at her side and kept her eyes peeled.

No Ruby.

Lily's palm sweat a little on the rosewood grip of her gun, so she discreetly switched it to her left hand, felt exposed as she swiped her right palm dry on the back of her shorts, and then got the gun back in her right hand, away from public view. Not that there was anyone on the path today. It was perfect beach weather, and though the bluff on the other side of the pines that ran the length of the bike path was too tall for any beach-goers to see her, she could hear them. The water sparkled between the trees, a blue jewel just out of reach.

She kept her right arm low and relaxed, close against her body. Her trigger finger itched, like it often did when she got the gun in her hand for target practice. She ignored it, inching along the patch of clipped lawn parallel to the bike path, breathing slow and steady.

In her practice sessions, her finger had always been on the trigger. It was the only way he'd take her seriously. He had to believe she'd shoot him. She had to believe it, too. But not yet. Not yet.

Ten or twelve yards ahead, the bike. Dumped on its side between two trees. That son of a bitch. He was nowhere. Neither was Ruby.

Lily turned toward the abandoned bike. Toward the lake. There was another patch of lawn on the beach side of the trees. She followed it. Once she had cover, she raised her gun to shoulder height, gripped it with both hands, and with her shoulders down and relaxed, pointed her gun and sighted a target that was not there. Not yet. But around or under the next tree, or the one after that. Had to be. She kept her finger off the trigger. For now. She drew a deep breath and put one foot in front of the other. Again. Again. Nobody. Not ahead. Not left. Not yet.

Three pines down, beach side, half under the long stiff branches, she found them. His pants were already down; he had Ruby pinned to the ground with his repulsive body. One hand held a knife against her neck. Lily eased her finger onto the trigger as he used his free hand to tug off Ruby's skimpy summer shorts.

Ruby, eyes widened in terror, saw Lily first. He turned to look, the knife digging into Ruby's throat. Lily saw blood. Her lower body didn't move, but her hands ticked the gun a fraction until it pointed right between his eyes.

"Get off her."

Instead, he pressed the knife harder against Ruby's neck, still looking at her. She glanced at the blood running down Ruby's neck, made sure the girl was not in the line of fire, and took her shot.

He dropped and her mind exploded with the gun, strobe flashbacks mixed with the present situation. Her blood. Ruby's blood. His blood. Ruby yelled one long howl as she scrambled out from under him, wildly pulling on her shorts. Lily allowed the arm holding her gun to drop, then went still. She'd shot to kill. And he looked damn dead, his brains sprayed all over the lawn, the tree, and poor little Ruby.

Lily carefully put her weapon away, pulled out her phone, dialed 9-1-1. Then she went over and tightly hugged Ruby. Her neck was cut and bleeding, but not profusely. She wasn't spurting. The knife must have been dull. Both of them shook harder than the trees blowing from the wind coming off the water.

After several minutes, Lily tried phoning Ruby's mom, Dr. Fass, but the line rang and rang. Finally she phoned Eddie and told him what had happened. Asked him to call his cop buddy. Asked him to come, too, to take care of Ruby.

****

By the time Eddie arrived, Harlan Tucker, chief of police and Eddie's good buddy, was at the scene. "We got us a justifiable homicide," he said, cutting away from the team of official looking folk behind the yellow tape. "Girl here"—Harlan hiked a thumb behind them at Ruby—"says she's your daughter. She gave me a statement, and I can release her to you if she's not just a crazy tourist. Got a scrape on her neck; EMT bandaged it up. Says she'll live."

"Ruby?" Eddie called. He was on the wrong side of the tape. He needed to get to her. It felt exactly like she was his daughter.

"Yep. That's her. She needs her momma real bad, but nobody at home is answering the phone."

"Her mom is Courtney." Eddie assumed Harlan knew which Courtney he was talking about even though Harlan was not a homeboy but had been hired and moved here from Detroit five years ago when Blue

118

Lake added a police station.

Harlan made a note. "Your wife, Courtney Fass?"

"That's right. She's Ruby Fass. It's complicated."

"She your daughter?"

Eddie avoided the question. "I'll take her home." Lily stood stoically in the background next to Ruby, her eyes on the distant water. Eddie thought Lily? Homicide? Somebody or something was covered with a green sheet. It almost blended into the lawn. What the hell? Had Lily's wild story been true then? There had never been a killing in Blue Lake. The kind of first that nobody wanted to claim.

Ruby had spotted him and hurled herself across the tape and into his arms. Harlan lifted the tape so she was on the public side. He'd decided to trust Eddie. And why shouldn't he? The man knew where he could be found, since they were in the same place every night when Harlan got off his shift and came into Eddie's place for a beer or two to wipe away the taste of the day.

Ruby was not weeping or dramatic except in that gesture. She buried her head in his chest and wouldn't budge, her arms clenched tightly about his waist.

"Where's your mom?" Eddie asked Ruby.

"I-I think at the new house. She said I could go to the beach and I met this guy…" She eased away from his body but kept her head pressed into his shoulder.

"Are you okay, honey?"

She finally looked up and nodded. "Lily saved me. He didn't get inside me."

Eddie winced. "Why isn't your mom answering her phone?" He didn't let his arm fall from her shoulder, not even to use his own phone.

The police siren started an abrupt wail as the ambulance loaded the body. After a brief exchange, both vehicles left, the cop car holding Lily full of noise and fury. The ambulance with the body beyond saving quietly exiting. Eddie looked around. The two of them were alone, everyone gone from inside the crime scene tape. Lily must have gone to the station with Harlan. He'd better call Bob.

"Let's get you home."

Once they were driving, Ruby said, "Mom lost the baby. It happened last weekend. She just got out of the hospital. There were…complications."

"She's okay?" Eddie wondered when exactly over the weekend. Had to be Sunday. After he'd given her those damned divorce papers.

"Pretending to be." Ruby answered his question with a strange lilt in her voice. She was keeping it together for him, he realized. He was grateful because he didn't know what to say to a teenage girl who had been assaulted and almost raped at knifepoint. He knew what he wanted to do to the guy who had done it, but Lily had already taken care of that.

Feeling ineffective, less than useless, he pulled up into the driveway of Courtney's new home. He couldn't let Ruby face her, tell her this, alone. He walked her up to the house and they stepped into the foyer. Courtney met them there. She'd clearly just woken up. Her phone was in her hand, the alarm still ringing. Ruby kissed her mom on the cheek, gave him a one-armed hug and headed up the staircase. "Shower," she said.

Eddie took the phone from Courtney's hand and turned the alarm off. Then he put it in the pocket of her robe. Courtney looked up at her daughter's retreating back.

"What happened?" Courtney scrubbed her face with her fists. "Why did you bring Ruby home?"

There were a couple of chairs in the foyer and Eddie led Courtney over to one. He was going to tell her straight and get the hell out of there. She was a shrink, she'd figure it out. "Ruby was almost raped today. Courtney, you have to get it together. This town is not the way it used to be. You can't let her run around on her own."

"What? When? Where?" She seemed genuinely stunned, ready to run up the stairs after Ruby. But they both heard the shower. "Is she okay?"

So she had heard him. "She is, but why are you still here? This seems like the worst place in the world for you two." He wondered if he should tell her about the knife or let Ruby explain that part herself.

"This is my home. With or without you." He saw grief sitting in her eyes. It felt bottomless. He listened for the shower. Still running. Ruby would need her mom to be strong. Could a person suffer and be strong? He shrugged. Life was suffering, pretty much.

He needed to leave. Somebody had to call Bob. So he changed the subject. "Are we divorced yet?"

He really didn't know how this worked. She shook her head. "You'll get final papers in the mail when it's over. But…"

"What?" He just wanted to be on his way.

"Hang on for a sec." She ran up the steps, ran back down, and handed the envelope to him. Same one he'd given her.

"She okay?" He knew she'd checked on Ruby. And the water was still running.

"She's not, but I heard her crying, so she will be. Thanks."

"She's a good kid. Music will help her. I will help her with music."

She simply nodded. Then took a breath and said, "I didn't send them. I couldn't…" He saw her straighten her spine, inch by inch. "Just—if you would—drop them in the mail. It's addressed and stamped."

They both heard the shower turn off in the silence that followed her statement.

"No problem," he said. And then he turned, envelope in hand, and walked out the door.

****

Bob, for once, was glad of his family's position in the town. Since Harlan was a family friend, the process of getting Lily out of the police station was over quickly. She'd made a signed statement, the particulars of which Bob was not privy to as of yet, but he did know she'd agreed to stay in town while the investigation was pending, and more importantly, she agreed to stay with Eva and Daniel. Bob had wanted to leave that house ever since he'd gotten home this summer, but if Lily was there, he was staying, too.

The four of them, including Eva and Daniel, said little in the car driving back to home base from the police station. Eva, Bob's sister-in-law, was like a second mom to Lily. Back before college, Lily had come to town, a runaway who landed in Blue Lake. Eva had not been married to Bob's brother, Daniel, then; she'd come to town to reopen her family's compound, the now semi-famous Blue Heaven. Blue Heaven, it could be argued, was the reason that tourists were turning the town into a place where things like rape and killing could happen. But that wasn't Eva's fault. Life was change. Bob knew that. Lily would not let him touch her, so he had to be content sitting by her side in the back seat of Daniel's Lexus.

If anyone could help Lily, it would be Eva. She'd taken Lily in five years ago, given her a roof and honest work, looked after her. Bob had tried to love her. But back then, Lily could not be loved. Even now, she would not let him comfort her. She shrugged Eva's hand off her shoulder when they got to the house. She said she just wanted to sleep.

Bob felt useless as usual when it came to Lily. But there was something he could do. He could find that mechanic, the one who had inspected Mrs. Van Slyke's car after the "accident." He remembered Lily saying he'd been good buddies with the guy she'd shot, her cousin. He could get a confession, not the one Lily wanted, but one that would satisfy her, maybe.

****

Lily lay on the bed in one of the many guest rooms on the Bryman mansion. She felt light and dark all at once. It confused her. She needed Dr. Fass. Only a doctor could understand that she was happy she killed him, but also horrified, the two emotions warred within her, polarizing her, setting off sparks like firecrackers: joy, remorse, sadness, guilt, freedom, ease, redemption, revenge, a dark black hole, like looking down the barrel of a gun.

A knock on the door. Bob. She didn't say anything, but he came in anyway. He would think he had the right now that they done the deed. Why had she done that again? Oh, the stupid plan. Her cousin hadn't said a word before she shot him.

"How you doing, honey?"

"I need Dr. Fass."

"Who? Courtney?"

"She's my shrink. You know I'm a little crazy, right? You need to get out of this relationship."

Bob didn't know Courtney was a shrink but whatever. He needed to get Lily back in the game. "I'll call her." He sat on the side of the bed, and she didn't push him off. A start. "I'm going to find the mechanic who inspected the car and said it was fine. We are going to get that confession. And this time I will not let you handle things alone. I should have been with you."

Lily didn't say that she had been avoiding him since they'd had sex. Sure, he'd been by the bungalow, but she had work to do with the reunion video and made excuses not to go out. She hadn't seen or talked to anyone in days. She'd needed some filler footage for the video, and that's the only reason she'd been hanging out in town when he saw him take Ruby. She didn't want to think about it. It was all she could think about.

"Okay," she said. "Please find him. But be careful. When my dad finds out what I did…"

"What? You stopped a rapist! He might have killed Ruby. If that knife had gone a hair deeper, she'd be dead instead of just traumatized. I guess it's good her mom is a shrink."

Lily had forgotten about that. Dr. Fass would be busy with Ruby. That was good. "Just be careful," she said, after telling Bob how to get to the mechanic's garage in her hometown.

Bob left on his mission, and she was alone. Truth was, she was scared. That's why she'd agreed to stay with Eva and Daniel. Her dad was not going to be pleased with this turn of events. He had never believed her about her cousin. Maybe he'd believe her now. Because of what had almost happened to Ruby. But somehow, she doubted it. He'd find a way to twist things and blame her. She wanted Dean.

Another knock on the door. Eva asking if she could come in. Lily didn't answer, and Eva turned the knob. Lily lay on the bed in the room letting the emotions flow. She'd had to trap her feelings inside for hours at the jail as she told her story, over and over. And just like he'd said at the crime scene, the police chief called it a justifiable homicide.

Justified, like the television show. There was no television in the room. Eva was apologizing about that very thing. Lily hadn't noticed. She felt the old quilt on her cheek. Eva loved old things. Odd comforts like the mug of warm tea Eva set on the beside table for her, urging her to drink.

Eva sat on the edge of the bed. The dent Bob had made was still warm. Hell was other people. Who had said that?

"Daniel called your father."

Lily shuddered. Somehow deep inside she felt her dad had been complicit in everything. A cohort. He didn't believe she was raped, he didn't believe Mom had been murdered, he had loved her cousin and not her, just because he was a boy, a man. Would he love the corpse more than his living, breathing daughter? Of course he would.

Eva pulled a blue flowered handkerchief from her pocket and gave it to Lily. She had not been crying, but tears leaked out of the corners of her eyes. She felt no remorse in this moment, but it would return, ping-ponging back in a minute or an hour. This had been her life since the rape, and she only felt whole when she was planning revenge, gun in hand. But she had never planned to shoot it at anything other than a paper target, only use it to force a confession. Who would believe her? Even she didn't believe it now. In that moment she had wanted to shoot him and she had. Simple awful truth.

"Bob's gone to find the mechanic who inspected your mom's car. He's bringing him back to make a statement, and he's going to find the car and have it reexamined, and I don't know what all else. Probably punch your father. Although Harlan, I mean Chief Tucker, asked Daniel to call your dad and tell him to come down here, not to say why, but that he was needed on an urgent matter regarding your cousin. He'll have to ID the body."

Eva gasped, realizing what she had said. "I'm so sorry, honey."

Lily shivered and Eva tucked a soft throw around her.

"I can call the doctor to come over and prescribe something for you, to help you sleep."

"No. I need Dr. Fass."

"Honey, you're in shock."

"Call her for me, please," Lily begged. "Tell her she can bring Ruby. Or not. Maybe not. I don't want Ruby to have to think about it. Never mind, I need to call Dean."

"Dean?"

"He's the guy who taught me to shoot. Not film, guns. He's an ex-cop. He can help Bob."

"Eddie's with Bob. They'll handle it. Drink your

tea, honey."

"Eddie is Dr. Fass's husband. Ruby told me. Can you call Dr. Fass?" Lily obediently sipped the tea. It was laced with whiskey and honey. "This is good. But I think I need some meds. Dr. Fass knows my other doc. We had a session when I first got to town."

"Shhh, honey, listen, Courtney, Dr. Fass, just lost a baby a few days ago."

"No!" Lily sat up and peered at Eva. Her eyes felt heavy and sore. "Bet that news spread through town quick."

"Everyone suspects the baby was Eddie's even though Courtney—Dr. Fass—has been in town less than a week."

"Well, I guess justifiable homicide will trump that lie."

"Honey, you didn't mean it. Bob told us your plan to force a confession. Of course we all believe you. That man you killed, he was a monster. You saved Ruby! If you were an officer of the law, that would be your sworn duty. In fact, Harlan was pretty impressed with you."

"Dean."

"Who?"

"Dean. Ex-cop who taught me to shoot. I need to speak to him. They kept my phone, didn't they?"

Eva was calling somebody on her cell, probably a doctor to give Lily meds, and probably not Dr. Fass.

Eva absently patted her and spoke quietly into her phone.

"I killed the bastard. He deserved to die. I'm fine it was me who did it."

Lily didn't care who heard her.

"Shhh." Eva hung up the phone. "I know."

"They'll say it was premeditated. I mean, I had a plan. It included a gun." Lily wondered what Dean would say. She just needed to hear his voice. "But Dean knows I never meant to kill a living thing. I wanted to protect myself from him and guys like him. They're everywhere. Especially at college. I didn't even know he was in town. He was stalking me! He took Ruby because he knew we were friends, kind of. I like the kid. So he showed me what can happen to things I like."

"That makes perfect sense to me. Here." Eva handed over her phone. "Call Dean. And call Dr. Fass to see if Ruby's holding up okay if you want to."

"Where is my dad going? To the cop shop? He's not coming here?" She scrunched her body around the phone and sobbed.

Eva was so sweet. She stayed and let her cry it out. Didn't take long. She needed Dean. Now.

"Drink your tea. It will calm you down so you can make your calls and then the doctor will be here with some meds."

Eva closed the door on her way out, but only after Lily picked up the ugly-ass old cup and finished the tea. It hit her stomach and eased things a notch. She set it down and called Dean. His cell rang and rang and then went to voice mail. She screamed and threw the phone across the room. Dean had promised to always take her calls. It took a few minutes for her to remember he would not know the number on his screen.

She peeled herself off the bed. Her body felt ancient, full of arrow wounds. She limped over to the phone. It had not broken, thanks so much. She had to control herself. She needed her shrink, and it really wasn't fair to Dr. Fass to call her right now, but if she could just remember some of the coping mechanisms. Close eyes. Roll pupils to top of head. Take deep, even breaths. Just a few. Okay. Call Dean again. Leave a message.

"Dean. It's Lily. I have a new phone. I got into some trouble with my gun. I shot him. I'm sorry. I didn't mean to, but he was…he was…call me." Scenes of the near-rape flashed in front of Lily's eyes as if she was there, on the bike trail. They mixed up with scenes from her own rape, just the way they did right before she shot him dead.

The phone rang in her hand. Dean.

"Post Traumatic Stress Disorder."

"Oh."

"Where are you? I'm coming. I'm already in my car. Got my trailer hitched."

"There's a state park where you can set up." This felt surreal. She needed him, and he was coming. "Thank you." She told him where to find her and then she hung up, relief flooding her body. She knew what to do now. Yes, PTSD. The flashbacks. The strobe and sparks. Did Dr. Fass know about PTSD? No matter. Dean was an ex-cop. He spoke their language. He would save her from his little silver trailer, the one he took on road trips to help with his own PTSD.

She didn't have her purse or her phone, what had happened to her phone? Evidence, because she'd kept the voice recorder part on even though nobody said anything and you really couldn't hear anything except her one shot and then Ruby being hysterical and Lily saying over and over, "You're okay, you're okay."

She needed her phone, damn it. She didn't know Dr. Fass's number by heart like she knew Dean's. She wanted to make sure Ruby was okay. With a shrink for a mom, she might be. And that dead bastard had never actually got inside her, didn't get as far as he had with Lily when she was maybe a year or two older than Ruby. Maybe Ruby would be okay. Lily would never be okay. Not now. Something happened to a person when they killed another person. Even an evil person who deserved to die. It changed you. She was changed. She wasn't like Bob and Eva and Daniel anymore. She was like Dean.

Being with Dean might help...being with Bob didn't anymore. She didn't know why. It was like he was too innocent. Dean had killed more than one scumbag. It made you different, he'd said once. Now she knew it was true. She'd rather stay in Dean's little silver trailer where they had talked the nights away than here in this mansion surrounded by people who loved her, but whom she could not seem to love back, no matter how much she tried.

Loving Bob like a normal girl had been her only goal, well, besides the big one, the confession. Poor Bob. She was goofed up about intimacy, had confused love with sex. Okay, be cool, she told herself. Bob knows you love him. Just not like that. Not like she loved Dean, even. But then, that was hopeless too. Two crazies do not make a sane.

Chapter Eight

Courtney came around to see Lily as soon as Ruby fell asleep. Her mom was there in case Ruby woke, but Courtney was pretty sure she'd sleep through the night. Lily might need her. She didn't know Eva well, but everyone knew the Brymans. She knocked on the big glass door so like her own. A blur that turned out to be Lily answered and almost dragged Courtney inside the house.

"Is Ruby okay?"

"Are you okay?"

They spoke at the same time.

"I'm feel like I'm under house arrest."

"You saved my baby! You should be given a medal!"

Eva led them into the living room, murmured something about tea, and left them alone. Courtney sat next to Lily on the mile long sofa and put her arm around the girl. Lily's entire body hummed with tension under Courtney's arm. "Did you have another flashback when you saw him on Ruby?"

Lily nodded. "And just a little while ago…I didn't tell the cops about my plan. They're going to find out, and they'll arrest me, and I'll go to jail, and my dad will be in court laughing at me when they lock me up and throw away the key!"

Lily was nearing hysteria by the end of the

sentence. "Breathe, Lily. It's the PTSD. Let's do the eye exercise. I'm going to talk while you close your eyes."

Lily's eyes fluttered. She was trying. Good enough. Courtney continued talking. The actual M.D. would be here soon with the prescription. Eva had made that call right after she'd talked to Courtney about what to do. "This is the PTSD. You've had it before, and this is another episode. Nobody is going to arrest you for anything. You saved my daughter's life today. Thank you."

"But, you're, but you just, I'm so selfish! You just lost a baby! Your daughter was almost raped by a beast. He killed my mother. I told you he did! See?"

"Lily, your eyes. Close your lids and listen to me. PTSD. I know your story. I know about the plan. You told me all about it. It's not a crime to think about ways to make someone own up to their atrocious actions." Lily's eyes stayed closed. "Good. Good. Now just roll your eyeballs up into the top of your head. Okay. Keep your lids closed. Yep, you're doing great. You're not selfish. You're not going to get into trouble. You have PTSD. You've had it before. You got through it. You'll get through it this time too."

Lily opened her eyes. Her breathing was easier. Courtney felt a wash of relief. It was good to help other people. It made her feel good not to focus on herself. She knew she needed to mourn for her baby, and she needed to be strong for Ruby. But right now, this felt like where she should be and what she should be doing.

"That's what Dean thinks too."

"Dean?"

Lily spilled the story out, the sparks, the confusion,

the ping-pong emotions, Dean and Bob.

Courtney listened. She owed this young woman her daughter's life. The so-called victim had a switchblade, a lethal weapon, less than an inch from her daughter's carotid artery. Not to mention strong hands that could smother or strangle. Not to mention rape. If he had killed Lily's mother, and Courtney thought this a true possibility now, there was no telling what he would have been capable of. From rape to murder was an escalation that changed the picture. She explained this in a few simple words, leaving the scariest parts out, to Lily.

Eva came in to the front room with tea things as the foyer bell rang. She set down a silver tray with china cups. "Help yourself," she said, then went to answer the door.

Courtney noted the black bag of a medical man before she looked up to a young face and sincere smile. Eva made introductions and then left for another teacup although nobody had touched the pot. Courtney explained the situation to Dr. Bell, filling in blanks when he asked a question. Lily was silent at her side, leaning into her. She kept her arm around Lily. Eva came in and poured tea all around, then picked up her own cup and said "I'll leave you to your session. I'll be in the morning room if you need me, Lily."

Then she left the room.

"Thanks, Eva," Lily said.

Courtney thought she may as well dive in with the good doctor.

"I am a licensed cognitive therapist in California, but here I'm just setting up a practice and am informally seeing Lily until I can decide how to hang my shingle."

"Okay, welcome. We need someone like you here. I need someone like you." He smiled again and Courtney felt relief. No California kook jokes. Not that she'd expect that of an M.D.

"So would you advise Xanax for the PTSD?" he asked.

"Yes," Courtney said, wanting one of those little blue pills herself. Just a reflex. She let it go. "It should help her sleep, too."

Dr. Bell called in another prescription and asked it to be delivered to the Bryman residence. They all sipped tea and nibbled cookies.

"He was a monster." They were the first words Lily spoke since Dr. Bell heard her story.

"I'm so sorry," he said, rising and gripping his bag. "You're in good hands here." He first addressed Lily, then turned to Courtney. "Please let me know if you need anything. Anything at all."

Since Courtney did not have the necessary credentials to prescribe medication, she often worked in consult with medical doctors and psychiatrists, who did. Dr. Bell was a lifeline for her and Lily both.

After the doctor left, Lily said, "Dean is more like a father to me than my own dad ever was."

"Do you remember a time when your father was loving toward you?"

"Yeah. Before I got breasts. After that, he ignored me."

"It's not uncommon for men of his generation to be uncomfortable with a daughter's sexuality."

"Oh, so you're going to defend him?"

"I'm wondering if you'll be able to repair the

relationship after this second rape attempt comes to light."

Lily laughed, a bitter sound. "I doubt it."

The bell rang again. Busy house. Eva came into the room with her wallet and paid for the prescription. She handed the bottle to Courtney. "Should I leave?"

"No, it's fine. Stay," Lily said, reaching for the pill Courtney handed her. "I'm used to these episodes. I had them in college. I know the signs."

And so did Courtney, although she didn't say anything. Her problems, and messy emotions, were on hold until she could help this young woman, and Ruby, through this nightmare. She had to be strong for the girls.

"So you're my shrink now, right? Like, officially?"

"Yes, of course. My methods are a little different than the norm. For example"—here Courtney looked at Eva, who seemed to be a mother substitute for Lily— "most therapists would not take on a patient who had just saved her daughter's life. Conflict of interest. But because I know Blue Lake, and Dr. Bell confirmed, there really is nobody else here to help, I want to do this."

Eva nodded. "It seems so odd that it be a conflict. It feels normal to me, to want to help, I mean."

Courtney nodded. "It's an ethics thing, but I'm not under any type of oath here. I can write my own rules."

"We have a connection," Lily said, grabbing Courtney's hand. "I don't care about rules either."

****

Dean drove straight through the six hours it took to arrive in Blue Lake from the southwest side of the state. He'd secured a spot on the park campgrounds even though it was high summer and the tourists were packed like ice in coolers. He pulled into town after dark, lit a lantern, and unhitched his little silver bullet of a trailer, angry with himself for not following up with Lily and her wild (or so they seemed at the time) accusations regarding her mother. God, what a dumb ass he'd been. Because of her neuroticism, he'd underestimated her instincts.

Her mental health issues had not stopped her from becoming a crack shot. No woman he knew held a revolver as steady, no trigger finger so sure as hers, no aim more accurate. Also, as he'd always damn well known, and she had now proven, that aim was deadly.

He didn't do much to set up camp, just unhitched, lugged out a ratty lawn chair and grabbed a beer for the ritual look-see. The beauty of his trailer—everything kept ready for a whim or a job. This was a bit of both. He'd established a connection with local law enforcement, but he wanted, was anxious for, was information on Lily's state of mind. She had good friends here. On the drive up he'd spoken not only to the police chief but to Eva Bryman, whom Lily had always talked about with much admiration and love. Eva said it was silly to stay in a trailer. The park was so noisy at this time of year. She had invited him into her home and, when he refused, offered him and his rig prime real estate she owned adjacent to the park.

Dean sipped from his beer bottle and craned his neck to scope the scene. A bonfire burned at the Bryman resort behind a stand of trees to the west. Waves of big water glittered in the moonlight to the north. Woods, dark and deep, stood to the south. Here and there, cottages plunked down close to the road, amid pines and scrub. The tents in the park were dark, all was quiet with the exception of teenaged murmurs emitting from a haze of marijuana smoke out by the bluff overlooking Lake Huron.

Dean finished his beer and got to his feet, snapping his chair closed and stowing it in the trailer. It was almost ten o'clock, but Eva had insisted he come by whenever he got in; Lily was anxious to see him. Dean didn't want to admit it, but he was curious about Bob Bryman. Lily had talked about the boy she loved and how she was going to win him back after college. Lily had no idea how easy it was for her to win a man's heart. Bob had likely held a torch for her the entire time they were apart.

Dean, disgusted by his stab of envy toward the younger man, got in his SUV and punched the address Eva had given him into his navigation system. Then he followed the blue line and the annoying voice to Lily's posh digs. He hadn't thought he'd ever see her again, and while this had pained him at the time, it was also a relief. In the years he'd known her, he'd come to care about her more than he should, given her vulnerable state, her adventures in bisexuality and promiscuity, and the large gap in their ages. He couldn't quite be her father, unless he'd been a teenaged dad. Biologically, he could be her father. Just not in line with his feelings, buried deep but still available in dreams and occasionally, like now, when his protective side flared.

He had been on a job out of the country at Christmas when Lily had needed him. And though they spoke on the phone, he had not been there for her. Off on a silly mission for a millionaire. Hell, it paid the bills.

****

Bob made sure he was the one to answer the door when Dean O'Malley knocked. Dean looked about his brother Daniel's age. They were alone as Bob ushered Dean inside with an exaggerated hand sweep he regretted as soon as it had been executed. Lily was sleeping, Daniel on the phone with the lawyers, Eva shopping online for things she thought Lily needed delivered overnight. So Lily's "friend," the guy "like a dad" to her, was not so old. Not so young either, but he had a full head of thick dark blond hair, deep lines at the corners of his eyes and biceps the size of hams.

The men eyed each other. Bob struggled to believe that though Dean might be older and experienced with firearms and protecting vulnerable people like Lily, he was no threat to their love.

The two shook hands, exchanged names. Dean's calloused grip was firm but not aggressive.

"Lily's sleeping. I'm on orders to wake her the moment you arrive." Bob motioned, more discreetly this time, for Dean to take a seat in the gigantic living room full of ornate oversized furniture. Not Bob's taste. He needed to get his own place. But he wouldn't leave without Lily.

"No need just yet. I'd like to ask you a few questions first, if you don't mind."

Bob couldn't imagine why this ex-cop, who hired himself out as a bodyguard and gave shooting lessons to college girls, thought he could do anything for Lily.

"Would you like something to drink?"

"Nope." Dean didn't sit. He paced, his long legs encased in ancient jeans. Looked like the guy had found his piece of carpet and meant to wear it out. Well, okay.

Bob got himself a beer and returned, sitting on the sofa.

"Shoot." Bob immediately felt a blush rise. Poor choice of words. Dean didn't seem to notice. He handed Bob his card. "Private Inquiry and Personal Protection" under his name, phone number under that. Three lines.

"Did you find the mechanic?"

"I did. He said he'd come in, make a statement, but he never showed."

"Did he tell you who paid him?"

"No. He said he wanted to make a formal statement to the police." Bob tamped down the defensiveness he felt building.

"And?"

Bob put down his beer and bit hard on a piece of skin hanging off the side of his thumb. He ripped it off. "Like I said. He never showed. Harlan, he's our police chief, went looking for the guy, but he's gone."

"I'll find him," Dean said. He didn't ask to see Lily, just turned around and let himself out the door.

Dread pooled in Bob's stomach. He had lost Lily when he lost the mechanic. And here was the badass from the big city come to save the day. He called Eddie at the bar.

****

"That Dean O'Malley fella's in town. Says he's gonna find the mechanic."

"Harlan will shit bricks over this." Eddie, his old phone jammed between shoulder and jaw, pulled a beer with one hand and talked with the other.

"I know where the mechanic lives," Bob said. "He's in the phone book."

"I'll be right over." Eddie served the beer and spoke to his manager. This was getting to be a habit.

"Lock up if I'm not back at closing time. And remind me to give you a raise." Charlene smiled. She was a damn fine bar manager. Not that he'd needed her or known she could handle things so well before a certain wife came back to town, necessitating all sorts of journeying from his favorite spot on earth. He gunned it over to the Bryman place.

Bob jogged out of the house and slammed into the truck. Eddie still had it in gear. "Just so I know—we're going after a guy to pin a murder on a dead man."

"For Lily." Bob finished the sentence.

Made total sense to Eddie. Bob had it bad for Lily, and Eddie knew something about that. He wanted Lily to get her confession too. If there was one to get. And if not from the dead man, from his mechanic. Also the idea of a flatlander coming in and solving Harlan's case (even though Harlan didn't think for one second that anybody killed Mrs. Van Slyke) didn't sit well with Eddie.

"You have to admit, it's weird how he disappeared."

Eddie didn't tell Bob that he didn't think Harlan looked too hard for the guy. But yeah, he thought it was a little weird. If the guy had nothing to hide, why run? He must have done the deed for the dead kid and so was technically a hit man.

When they'd paid him a visit earlier, he'd claimed no knowledge of any car tampering until Eddie said (lied, rather) that Harlan was having the vehicle impounded and it would be tested by state-of-the-art crime scene technology for any sort of fancy tampering. Bob had blurted out the evaporating water theory, and the mechanic had dropped his wrench.

"I'll come in, but I didn't do anything," he'd sworn. "Hell, there's twenty guys from here to Blue Lake who work on Caddies."

"Yes, but only you work on Mrs. Van Slyke's car." Bob was like a dog with a stuffed toy. He was going to work this guy until he shredded him.

"Yeah, and I inspected it after the accident. I got my own high tech methods, and I'm telling you, no foul play. Not even the thing the kid cooked up." The mechanic directed his reply to Eddie, smirking at Bob before he picked up his greasy tool, composure regained.

But that evaporating water trick was genius. The stuff of urban legend. It would work, sure, but Mrs. Van Slyke's car had swerved and hit a utility pole on the opposite side of the road. How could the mechanic ensure that happened? Had to be a conspiracy of dummies. Well, they'd almost gotten away with it. Almost.

"I talked to Lily today about that thing at the crossroads, where Mrs. Van Slyke swerved and ended up on the wrong side of the road."

"And?"

"Turn here. Okay, third house down. Top floor. Stairs around back." They parked in front of the mechanic's house. Too many cars and trucks on this street to know if one was his or not. "So, Mrs. Van Slyke had a hair appointment every Tuesday at 11 a.m. for twenty-five years. The cousin would know this. He could have set something up."

"I hate to say it, but it sounds far-fetched. Bet the guy will be home. Drunk. Forgot to visit the police. Missed Harlan's call."

They went up the back steps. The door was locked. Eddie knocked. No answer. He pulled out a credit card and popped the cheap lock. Why bother?

The place was a tip. Stacked empty pizza boxes left a smell that permeated the premises. A trash bin full of beer cans sat next to the fridge. A plastic garbage bag full of paper plates was kicked to the side of the sink. The other rooms were equally uncompelling. From the piles of dirty laundry in the bedroom, it didn't look like the mechanic had packed for any vacation.

"You realize Harlan doesn't think the cousin killed Lily. He's not interested in this mechanic."

"But Dean seems to think Lily may be right and so does Dr. Fass, er, Courtney."

Bob stopped by a plastic table next to a cheap leather-like chair. That and the huge television hung on the wall made up the bulk of the living room. "Look at this."

Eddie took the pad of paper with the garage's logo on top from Bob. "A street name." Bob was already looking at his phone, punching keys and swiping the screen the way kids did these days. "It looks like there's nothing there. A hundred acres of hunting land."

"Wait, I know that land." Eddie had looked around a lot before deciding to buy the property on the Sapphire River. "And guess who owns it?"

Bob rubbed his face. The kid looked tired.

"Papa Van Slyke," Eddie said.

Bob, alert now, nodded. "Interesting. Hunting cabin on the property?"

"Shit if I know. Let's go find out."

"Seems like a dumb place to hide."

"Not if nobody official seems very interested in

finding you."

"Okay." Bob closed the door on the way out.

They found the road and about half a mile in a two-track pathway. Bob shined the flashlight in the dark, but they didn't see any cabin. Still they kept riding. Eventually they saw a truck with the name of the garage on the side. "Bingo," Bob said.

The place was dark, but then it was after midnight.

They walked right into the place, door unlocked. Bob led the way, and Eddie almost walked into him because Bob stopped just inside the door, his flashlight trained on a dead body on a fancy carpet. The mechanic. His head was split open and congealed blood pooled underneath him. Just as they heard a car engine, Eddie noticed no blood had seeped anywhere except onto the rug. Shit.

Bob and Eddie stood there, Eddie dialing Harlan, hoping this new guy getting out of a plenty roomy SUV was not the one who had come to roll the body up and cart it away. Bob flashed his light. "That's Dean."

"The ex-cop Lily knows?" Eddie had already hung up with Harlan. Dean came up to the door, took in the scene, and used his own phone to call Harlan. He spoke too low for Eddie to catch his words. But it seemed as if Harlan had let him in on the case. Whatever. He didn't know what he was doing here except that Lily reminded him a little bit of Courtney at that age. Angry. Lost. Artist who didn't understand what she was yet.

Bob made introductions as the three men stood there not touching anything, waiting. Eddie was impressed with the ex-cop's detecting skills. He and Bob knew the area, knew the story, had been working on this thing for Lily all day. Dean had found it in what? An hour?

"Well, boys," Dean said, "looking at this as an outsider, I'd say the cousin didn't kill the wife after all."

Eddie and Bob were silent a beat. Eddie's mind went through the information like a stack of index cards. He was missing a few of them, but Bob caught on fast enough.

"Papa Van Slyke," Bob said. "Had to be. He's got a meeting with Lily tomorrow. Dr. Fass, I mean, Courtney, thought it would be good for closure."

"That'll work," Dean said.

"What?" Bob said over the sound of another engine running up the road. Just as quickly the vehicle rammed into reverse and got the hell out of there.

"The cleaner," Dean said. "Van Slyke may have done the killing, but he would want someone else to get rid of the evidence. A professional."

Damn. This guy was good. Eddie felt a little sorry for Bob. He'd been trying so hard to help Lily and be her hero, and now this guy shows up out of nowhere.

"Maybe the tire tracks will help the investigation," Bob said.

Dean smiled kindly. "Not likely to be found. But Lily had that plan and it takes the DNA lab a few days to get a match, if they find anything they can use, hair, fibers, blood."

"Lily said her dad's coming over at one. After lunch," Bob said.

"That'll give her plenty of time to set her trap," Eddie said, all the index cards finally lining up in his mind.

Bob nodded. Dean didn't say anything, but he

nodded too. Eddie had a feeling it was going to be a long night.

Chapter Nine

Lily's father pulled up five minutes late. That was fine. Somehow—slow news day? Dr. Fass magic?—there were reporters in the street. They took photographs of Papa like he was a celebrity. It sickened Lily. She plastered a fake smile on her face, remembering she wasn't alone. She had a team. Their plan was solid. The entire room was wired with videocams and voice. Lily had hidden them in strategic locations and had, after much deliberation, decided Papa's weakness was still going to be bourbon. Beside an old-fashioned crystal decanter on a bar cart from the 1920s, she aimed her best camera, disguised in the cocktail shaker, directly at the chair she intended to herd him toward. Around the shaker, soda, a carafe of wine, and assorted bottles filled out the tableau. But a Waterford bucket full of ice and the bourbon was the knife that would loosen the taut thread of Papa's lies. Her cameras, stashed on the mantel, on a table, in that cocktail shaker, caught every angle of the room. She'd finally have her confession.

When she'd first heard that her father had killed her mother, Bob breaking the news while Dean stood stoic at his side, something clicked. It made terrible sense. She was all in from the moment she saw the idea of a revised plan in Dean's eyes. Not that any of it would be admissible in court, but YouTube was a power unto itself. And Lily just needed to hear him say the words. Like she'd needed to hear her cousin. She had a moment of anxiety. What if this turned out like that? No. It wouldn't. There was a clear plan here. It was different. Dean was in charge. Bob was behind her, all the Brymans were. And her gun was still with Harlan Murphy.

Dean and Daniel had skills and resources Papa wouldn't be prepared for—her father (she hadn't called him Papa in years, but the name had stuck and now everyone else did) didn't know one thing about Dean, who was parked at the kitchen table, his laptop monitor watching everything in the room. Dr. Fass was here too. She'd coached Lily on how to handle the hypothetical conversation with her father. She'd also arranged media interviews after the meeting. Everyone, local and national, wanted an exclusive with Lily.

Lily's team had advised she stick close to the Bryman property and offer "no comment" and she had done so. No reason for Papa to think she'd go rogue once he pulled out of the driveway after their talk.

Dr. Fass was facilitating a "healing" process between Papa and Lily. What a joke, but it got him here. He wanted to look cooperative. He didn't know she knew they'd found the mechanic's body at his hunting cabin last night, that DNA evidence had been collected and put on fast track with state and local authorities.

"I'm afraid of him. Really afraid." Lily gave Dr. Fass one final look as Papa walked up the wide steps to the Bryman manse.

Just an hour earlier, Dr. Fass had asked how her father had come to be known as "Papa" to all the world.

"I used to call him that—before—"

"The rape?"

"Yeah."

"Okay, good. We can use that. It might trigger something in him." So Lily started thinking of her father as Papa again.

"Own that fear you feel. Use it," Dr. Fass said, opening the door.

"Hi, Papa." Lily smiled as cameras clicked. *Remember how close you once were; remember how you adored him,* Dr. Fass had counseled. Lily took her father's hand and pulled him into the big room, leading him past the bar cart with the bourbon clearly labeled on an engraved silver insert. Dr. Fass disappeared up the staircase, as they'd discussed. Lily ignored the bourbon on the cart and chose a bottle of water, setting it off to the side as she lifted a cut crystal glass, tossed in a few glittering ice cubes from the ice bucket, and asked her father if he'd like something. She tried to remember not to think of him as Dad or Father or Monster, but Papa.

"Small batch?"

"Hmmm?" Lily pretended not to know what Papa was talking about. He took the glass from her hand and lifted the stopper from the decanter. Poured generously. She picked up her bottle of water, twisted the top, and drank straight from the bottle as she headed to the sofa.

"Let's get this charade over and done," Papa said. He sat in a leather wing chair as far as possible from the sofa where Lily stood, pretending uncertainty. It was the spot where she'd aimed the cocktail shaker. He was a predictable man.

"It's not a charade to me," Lily said. "I want to

apologize for—for—" She wasn't acting. This was hard to say.

"For murdering your cousin in cold blood?" Papa took a large swallow of his drink. The glass never left his hand.

"Yeah, that." Tears sprang, and she let him see them. "I—lost it for a minute." She set her water bottle on the side table where another camera was hidden in a lamp. She'd be sick if she took another sip. "Papa…" She let the name hang in the air for a second or two. "Do you know why he was here?"

"I don't know shit except you killed him."

Lily didn't bother to correct his characterization of the scenario.

"Where's the family? Where's this shrink?"

"The family are out. My therapist thought it best if we had privacy, so we wouldn't feel inhibited by her presence." It was true. Dean was in the kitchen, monitoring the room with a laptop. The family were all out in the back, safely tucked into a garage office.

"So we're alone?"

"It's okay." She laughed, nervous. "The police still have my gun."

"Oh, I'm not afraid, little girl. But you should be."

She noticed the slight bulge under his jacket. Holster. He'd called her "little girl," which meant her act was working. He stood and went over to the cocktail trolley for another drink. Not unsteady on his feet. Yet.

"I am, a little," she admitted. Let him think he had the upper hand, and anyway, it was true.

He strolled over to the fireplace, resting an elbow on the mantel. Yes, he was a big man. Tall and intimidating. But Lily didn't feel intimidated anymore.

She felt something else. Anger. She waited until he took a healthy slug of his drink, then pounced. "Did you kill Mom?"

Papa swallowed, but his eyes bulged with the effort not to spew or cough. He left the drink—almost empty—on the mantel and marched toward her, roaring, "What did you say?"

"You heard me." She kept her tone soft and matter-of-fact. "See, I've had time to think about it and now that they found the mechanic's body—"

Papa choked. His face turned red. "When? How do you know that?" He stopped in the middle of the floor. "You're lying."

"In the cabin."

Papa grabbed his glass and filled it so full it sloshed over the rim and onto the rug as he walked to the sofa, sat, and faced her. He ignored the mess he'd made and she did, too.

"It's not what you think, Papa. I want to know because of what I did. Are we, is there something different about us? That we can kill people? Shouldn't I feel bad? Do you, Papa?" She looked at him through adoring eyes, the ones that believed he knew the answer to every question in the universe.

He drank. Good. "She was going to divorce me."

"No! She wouldn't!" Lily's surprise was real. Her mom had not said a word to her about any divorce.

He nodded. "Yep. That business with your trust."

"I understood about that—I told her I did. Her money is your money. Any lawyer knows that."

"Well, yes." Papa relaxed, his legs unbending, his fingers unclenching. He gave her an assessing look. "You're more like me than I realized."

She smiled, happy little girl being praised by her beloved Papa. "So it's okay not to feel bad?" But she did feel bad. Not that her cousin was dead, not exactly. But that he'd somehow ruined her for Bob. He'd made her different from other people. She'd killed someone and when you did that, you changed inside. It wasn't that she'd gotten cold or ruthless or insane. Just different. Outside the circle of normal.

"Guilt is a wasted emotion," Papa said, draining his glass again and glancing at his watch. He put his hand in his pocket, and Lily held her breath. What if he killed her right here? Right now? But Dean wouldn't let that happen. Papa pulled out a cell phone.

"Our little reconciliation scene has gone well, but I've got business."

Yes. The mechanic. He'd have to figure a way out of that one. He would. He always did.

Damn. He was phoning his driver. "Can you open the gate at the back?" he asked, but it wasn't really a question. He'd expected her to do this for him. Then he spoke to the driver. "Pull in when you see the gates open. I'll come out the back."

Double damn! No confession and he was heading into the dining room, straight toward the kitchen at the back of the house. And Dean.

Lily hurried to the arch opening into the dining room and grabbed her father's arm. "Papa, wait." They were still in camera range. Just.

He shook her hand off his arm, but he stopped. He patted her shoulder. She tried not to shudder.

"I just wish you could stay longer, that's all." She pulled at his hand, hanging back. If he left video range, voice range, all of it would be lost, a waste. Part art, part truth, zero result. Papa had not killed the mechanic. Someone else, someone professional and probably out of the country by now, had done that.

"Need to use the facilities?" She'd try anything to keep him from leaving camera range.

"I'm good."

"Your driver hasn't pulled through the gate yet."

"Well, you need to open it for me. Where's the keypad?"

"I, uh, they told me, and I'm trying to think…" She pressed the heel of her hand to her forehead. "I've been medicated."

"They've got you well protected. You may get off with a slap on the wrist. Powerful friends with too much money. I should have such problems. You did well, little girl. Probably keep your gun in the pocket of those blue jeans, huh?"

Eyes down, she nodded. "When I have it." She turned slightly so she wouldn't block the camera on the mantel. It was nestled into a hollowed out wooden owl. "I'm sorry Papa—not for killing him—he took my place in your heart." Ha. Like he had one. "And for that, well, it's like I said, I can't feel sorry he's dead."

"No great loss," Papa said. But he stayed. She knew he liked flattery. Almost as much as bourbon. The stuff should be working on him by now. Loosening his tongue. Think, Lily. What could she say to get him to spill? He'd been crazy about her cousin. Why would he say it was no great loss?

"Mom was a loss to me," she said.

"I already told you why I did it. She was going to leave. Sue me."

He didn't seem to realize that he'd just admitted to

murder. She was sure the owl caught it.

And then he was gone, out the back door, Dean and his laptop disappeared. She ran outside for one last look, and to see if Dean was out there. Her father, no need for the Papa charade anymore, had never seen him. But still. She didn't want them to meet.

The tinted window glided down. "When you get your gun back, be careful not to shoot your ass off," her father said. He laughed, and she tried for a rueful grin. Dean stood by the door and used a subtle thumbs-up to punch the code from the garage wall. The minute the taillights cleared the wrought iron gates, he led her into the house.

"He's got some scrambling to do," Dean said. Lily smiled.

After she'd freshened up inside, she came out back, where the gates were now open and the family sat behind a bank of wide tables. Dean escorted her to a chair near the middle, next to Bob. He sat on her other side. Dr. Fass was there. Ruby, too, brave girl. A guy Dr. Fass knew from her other life was making preliminary statements. Lily would answer no questions until her exclusive interview with a national magazine, directly after which she had another interview on live local television. She felt like she had to do this stuff for Dr. Fass and the Bryman family. For Ruby. Everyone could get closure, Dr. Fass said. Lily just wanted it over.

Dr. Fass answered a few questions, just general things about PTSD and how Ruby was doing. Dean played the voice part of the taped confession. He didn't explain where it came from, but everyone in town knew Lily was a videographer. It was not a felony to practice your craft. And the questioners had stopped calling her a "shooter." She was now a young woman who had avenged her mother's death and stopped the rape of an innocent girl. She was a hero. But she didn't feel like one. She felt empty. Numb.

****

Bob watched as Dean pulled out of the state park next to Blue Heaven. He sat in the gazebo above the lake, waiting for Lily. She'd been avoiding him, had moved back into the bungalow last night but then asked to see him this morning. There was one highway that led out of town, and Dean was on it. Somehow, it didn't lessen the tension in Bob's gut. Dean headed west, toward Lake Michigan. He didn't wave good-bye.

Lily came out just as Dean's tail lights were fading from view.

"It's not what you think with him," she said, sitting next to Bob and taking his hand.

"I don't think anything. I don't know what to think. You need time. I love you. I can wait." He knew he had to shut up or lose her. She already seemed gone, far away with her own thoughts, looking out to the big water. Which had been the moment he'd lost her? When she shot the gun? When Dean got to town? Before? He'd never ask, never know. Maybe, if she stayed, someday…

"I'm leaving," she said. "Gonna chill someplace random for a bit."

He nodded because he couldn't speak. He watched her walk away, get in her car, and head down the same highway Dean had just disappeared into. With a shiver of relief, Bob noted that Lily turned east instead of west.

154

Chapter Ten

When Courtney was a little girl, she'd been playing tag, fallen onto a tin can and cut her knee. It didn't hurt. Her skin opened up, split in two, looked like peanut butter and jelly all the way across her leg, just under her knee bone. A few of the girls screamed and ran home. Other kids helped her cross the street to her own house because her leg wasn't working right.

Her mother had been at the grocery store, so her dad had to take her to Doc for stitches. Thirteen of them. That didn't hurt either. Not even when Doc gave her a shot. What hurt was having to stay on the front porch and watch the other kids play. She lasted a day. Two. But, on the third day, the tension was so great it made her move. She jumped up and went across the road to Cheryl Tanner's house. Cheryl's dad had just put up a fence, a wood one, with a top the size of a balance beam like Courtney had seen on the Olympics. It was three feet tall and none of the kids could walk it. Courtney just knew she could balance, stitches or no.

And she had walked that fence until Old Man Tanner came out and yelled at her to get off his goddamn fence. He yelled so loud she fell again. That broke a couple of stitches, but it didn't hurt. Her mother shrugged and dabbed at the beads of blood with cotton and peroxide.

"What am I going to do with you?"

"Mom, I can't stay on the porch all summer."

Her mother had kissed Courtney's head. "I know, baby."

Courtney was not a baby. But she didn't protest. Her mother had given silent approval for play to resume. Within a week, she'd broken every stitch. She even pulled them out herself because they were gross and stiff with blood. She still had the scar. It was silver now, and the faint traces of the stitches were there too, to remind her that she was tough. She didn't hurt easy.

But here she sat, in the same room Doc had once slept in with his wife, and she didn't feel tough. She'd gotten through the ordeal with Lily. Ruby had the same stuff as Courtney; her girl was tough, too. They'd both been okay as long as they were helping Lily. Now Ruby was pretending to be okay, but a trial was pending because the DNA evidence was conclusive: Papa Van Slyke had killed the mechanic. He'd hired a cleaner, but before the guy could get there, the three civilian men, Lily's protectors all, had shown up. And Papa had pulled the trigger himself. There wasn't going to be a second count for killing his wife, even with the confession splashed all over the internet and print papers. The YouTube sensation made front page news, and possibly Lily's career, but it was inadmissible in court.

Lily was not being charged with a crime, and Harlan had given her permission to leave town, as long as she stayed in contact. There was still the matter of the family fortune, and it was unclear if that would become part of the case against Papa Van Slyke or simply be ironed out by lawyers. Courtney didn't know where Lily had gone. Nobody did. Lily had promised she would call Ruby when she settled somewhere. So that was Ruby's focus, still, days later. "I wonder if Lily will call today."

Courtney glanced at the clock. Three a.m. Of course. It was like her body knew when Edward was heading home. Ruby had not mentioned Edward, not since Courtney had burst into tears the day Lily left town, and Ruby wondered if they could stop in for a burger and say hi. The tears had surprised Courtney, who was always strong for her daughter. Always. Without fail. Except that once. Ruby had turned white under her summer tan. "Never mind, Mom," she'd said. "Who needs that old coot anyway?"

Courtney laughed because Ruby never used words like "coot." Or she pretended to laugh, and choked back the tears and wondered what the hell was happening to her. She only let herself think of Edward after Ruby was asleep. She read the letter, over and over, the one he'd written her when they were kids.

In a way, it helped her get over the baby. It helped her cope with Ruby's horrible experience. Now that she was out of therapist mode and back to being Mom, she was having a hard time. For the first time in a long time, she remembered what hurt felt like. And she couldn't keep peanut butter and jelly in the house.

So Edward was a coping mechanism. Nothing more. Fantasies of what might have been kept her from other, worse, might-have-beens. She traced events backward. He'd gone off her because of the lie. About the baby. It had been a terrible lie. She didn't know the part of herself that was capable of telling such a lie. She understood Edward's horror. She had to forgive herself for that lie. She worked on it a little bit every day. It hurt worse than a busted stitch, worse than peroxide on raw skin, but she held herself in compassion for what she had lost. Why couldn't Edward hold her in compassion, too?

If Edward forgave her, if they could become a family, it would help Ruby. Her daughter would feel secure, she'd have music and laughter and a man around the house. Yes, Edward should forgive her for Ruby's sake, at the very least. She glanced at the letter, puckered with dried tears. She knew every word by heart. They were all lies.

Stop it, she told herself. But then she remembered how she'd called Edward every day since Ruby had been assaulted. She'd texted him. And he had not returned her calls or texts or in any way acted as if she were a person living in the world. Living in a world of hurt for a long time.

Maybe she didn't know Edward at all. Maybe it had all been false, right from the start. She was confused; she should be able to figure this stuff out. She had a couple of degrees in human psychology, after all. Turns out, she didn't know as much as she thought she did. All she knew how to do was be kind. She was very kind to Ruby. She even treated herself, when she remembered, with kindness.

And she knew, deep inside, that she would never ever heal until she could think of Edward with kindness too. She had to forgive him for not loving her. She couldn't quite do it yet, but she would get there. As soon as she didn't need someone to blame for her ruined life anymore, she'd forgive him. As soon as the pain went away, the baby pain, the Ruby pain, the Lily pain. As soon as that faded, she could erase the Edward pain and not even leave a scar.

****

Eddie wiped down the bar and then buffed it to a shine for the final time that night. Three nights since Lily had left town. Two nights since he'd seen Courtney's face on the television set. One night since he'd imagined Ruby being raped and lost his ability to count change. She hadn't been raped. That was what he had to remember so he could hand dollar bills back to his wait staff.

He didn't think about those calls and texts and things. Had erased them all without even looking at them. He'd been alone too long, and he liked it that way. He didn't need a house full of women around with their rose colored walls and flowered furniture. Ruby would be fine. If Courtney couldn't cure her own daughter, well, Courtney could. She was a tough broad. The toughest.

As his staff filed out one by one, nobody asked about Ruby. This was the first night not one person had said her name. Not even a customer. Not to him, anyway. Hungry vultures had not left him alone since the shooting. It was better if he could say he didn't know how Ruby was and leave it at that. It was better he not get mixed up in all that mess. Let the Brymans deal with it. Let Courtney's family help. Eddie didn't want any part of it. He couldn't even bring himself to drop those damn divorce papers in the mail. They stared up at him from the bottom of his safe every night when he prepared the bank deposit.

Tonight was no different from any other night of his life. He hung the wet towel to dry on a hook he'd hammered for just that purpose, locked up and pulled the cash drawer out of the old-style register he refused to replace. It felt so heavy. Either he was feeling his age, or the vultures were making him rich. He took the drawer into the office.

He opened the safe and ignored that damn envelope the same way he ignored Courtney's texts and phone calls. He was good at ignoring stuff. Had a lifetime of practice. Courtney was not the first persistent lover he'd had to shake loose.

She might be the last. He finished up just as the delivery bell rang at the back door. He looked out the security camera and saw his buddy, Harlan Tucker. He went out and let the chief of police in, locking the door behind them.

"Thought I'd check in," Harlan said, moving into Eddie's office and taking a seat on the sofa. Eddie had gotten used to Harlan's semi-regular check-ins at closing time. He was not in uniform, so it was really a social call. Sometimes Harlan didn't sleep so well. Went with the territory, he'd told Eddie one time early on in their friendship. Eddie took a beer from his personal fridge. "Frosty mug?"

Harlan laughed, opened the twist off top of his beer, and drank deep.

"No frosty mug necessary, but thanks."

"For what?" Eddie wheeled his rolling office chair out from behind the desk and put his feet up on the other end of the beat up old sofa.

"The offer. The beer."

Eddie nodded, wondering what was on Harlan's mind. Working behind a bar had taught him that if you just kept your mouth shut, pretty soon someone else would open theirs. That had always been true of Harlan.

This early morning, Harlan didn't seem in a hurry to do much talking. He took another long pull of his beer.

"What's up?" Eddie couldn't help himself. He was pretty sure the entire thing with Lily and Ruby and Papa Van Slyke was as done as it was going to get for a while, but you never knew. If there were developments, he wanted to know. The realization shocked him and while Harlan drank more beer, Eddie silently wondered why he cared. Shit. He cared.

"Nothing my end. Just doing a check-in. You?" Harlan set his half-finished beer on the tiled floor.

Eddie didn't know what to say. Something big had just happened, but it was invisible. Maybe Harlan hadn't noticed. "Not a thing."

"Seen anything of young Ruby?"

"No. Why?" Eddie knew that was too abrupt but he was very busy zipping up his feelings, which had decided to take control.

"Well, I thought you were going to help her get onto *American Music Star* or something. You were gonna teach her stage presence. She was your newest protégé. As far as I recall." Harlan picked up his beer again and drank a slow sip, like he had all night.

"Well, yeah, I was going to," Eddie sputtered, "but now I don't think it's such a good idea. Her mother…" He trailed off, unwilling to get into this shit. He had to think about it some more.

"You said she had talent. You said she could be great. You said she needed proper guidance." Harlan eyeballed him in that way cops had, like they could see inside every lie, even the ones you told yourself. "And I remember something about how it would be great for her to have something to focus on besides almost being raped and murdered."

Eddie winced. He felt a jab of physical pain so strong, it took his breath for a second.

"What? I say something out of line?"

"No. You're just reminding me of what a dumb ass I've been." Eddie wasn't sure if he'd been a dumb ass for ignoring Courtney and Ruby or if he'd been a dumb ass to get involved with them in the first place.

"Oh? How so?"

"I don't know." Then out came the story of the pregnancy, Xander's visit, the miscarriage, the divorce papers, the entire messy wad of life that had suddenly spilled into his neat, clean life.

Harlan listened. He'd make a good bartender. After Eddie finished, Harlan didn't speak for a minute. He pondered while Eddie stewed. Then, finishing off his beer, Harlan belched discreetly, opened a half full case of empties that doubled as a coffee table, and set the bottle inside. He closed the lid. "You love her?"

"Who? Ruby?" Did he? He cared, but did he love? Did he even have the capacity to love anymore? What was love? He wanted, had wanted Courtney as a woman. Had wanted to help Ruby achieve her musical dreams.

"Both of them. They're a matching set." Harlan interrupted Eddie's train of slippery slope logic.

"Hell, I don't know. I don't know if there is such a thing as love."

"There is. I see it every day in my line of work."

"I see a lot of drunk people acting like fools in mine."

Harlan just nodded.

Does wanting plus caring equal love? Eddie didn't know.

"Tell me about this so-called love you see every day."

"I see the love a woman has for a man when he's had a heart attack on the job and I have to go tell her he's in the hospital. I see the love a man has for a woman when another man tries to take her away and he beats the shit out of the guy. I see the love a parent has for their child when the kid's being bullied and they come to the station for advice. I see the love a parent has for their child…"

"Okay, okay, I get it." It seemed that caring about another person, about their well-being, was in fact a component of love. "I might love them. I care about them."

"That's love, you dumb ass."

****

After Harlan left, Eddie let himself out the back door, locked up. He did the bank drop, slowing as he approached Courtney's street. Her light was on upstairs, just like it was every night. What was wrong with him? Only one way home but why was he slowing down, setting his foot gently on the brake? Why was he turning his head and glancing down her block?

Why then did he turn onto her road? What made his foot hit the gas pedal a little harder, speeding toward her, the love of his life, his wife, soon to be ex if he ever got up the courage to take those damn papers to the mailbox. He pulled in front of her place, cut the lights, turned off the engine, pulled out his cell phone.

"You called?" He said it like she'd phoned just a minute before, instead of forty-seven hours and twenty minutes ago. She'd answered right away. He listened to her breathing. He watched the light in her bedroom.

"Oh."

That was all she had to say? Now what?

"How's Ruby?"

"Fine. She'll be fine."

"You?"

"Good."

"That's a damn lie." He didn't know what was wrong with him. He couldn't think of the right words to say.

"Where are you?"

"Look out your window."

He saw the curtain move, saw the shadow of her face. Her face. He needed to see her face. "Want company?"

Chapter Eleven

Courtney felt hope rise but tamped it down. Maybe if she told Edward it would make a difference. Or maybe that would be wrong. She'd have to wait and see. It was a good sign that he'd showed up at this time of night, wasn't it?

"Okay. Come on in."

"Is your door not locked?"

She chuckled. It surprised her that she could laugh, even a little bit. "You kidding? In this town?"

"It's not the same town," he said. He was dead serious. "Too many strangers these past few summers."

She watched him slide his long legs out of his truck, watched him start the walk to her door, had to stop herself from skipping down to meet him. She'd questioned the nurse after Ruby left about the panic attack. Was it so common as the nurse seemed to believe? Or was she only trying to calm Ruby down?

"Hi." She peeked up at him and his open face, so full of love, made her feel hopeful but still unsure. He'd fooled her with that look a few times already these past weeks. "You sure do pick a peculiar time to pay a social call."

"Well, as I recall, you prefer early morning visits."

They smiled at each other, shy as kids.

He accepted a seat on her sofa and the offer of a glass of water. She went into the kitchen to get them drinks, pouring herself a half glass of wine. What the hell. It might give her courage.

Turns out, that nurse had informed her, most women who had their ovaries removed, and every other one of their female parts, slammed directly into menopause, leaving them without the vital hormones the body had been accustomed to since the onset of puberty. This often caused a single episode of panic. Nothing that would come back, the nurse, and Courtney's subsequent research, had assured her. Her mother had been the one to sign the release forms. Next of kin, of course. And she reminded Courtney that two of her aunts had died from ovarian cancer. One was a great aunt, and Courtney had many living aunts, but she saw her mother's point. If they were going in, might as well take it all.

She brought the drinks in and handed Edward his. Then she sat on the opposite end of the sofa. It was a very long sofa. She had probably bought it thinking of Edward's legs stretched out on it. The subconscious was a tricky thing.

"So." He looked at her glass of wine. She remembered how she had not sipped even that one glass that first day. She'd done research on that too, trying to find a reason to blame herself for the miscarriage and the ensuing hysterectomy. "I'm sorry you lost the baby."

"It's okay. Wasn't meant to be." She swallowed a demure sip.

"Who knows? You might have another some day."

"No. That part of my life is over." She couldn't do it. She couldn't say the words.

"Now, Court…" He set his glass of water carefully

on a coaster and was by her side, holding her, in an instant. "If that's what you want…"

She wasn't sure she heard him right, but the story of the surgical removal of her female organs came tumbling out just the same. She sobbed into his checked shirt. It smelled like starch, just a little bit. She wiped her tears with her hands and reached for a tissue to finish the job.

"Sorry. I still get emotional about it all."

"I hope you don't blame yourself."

"Only off and on, every five minutes."

"Shhh. You shouldn't."

He continued to hold her and she put her head on his shoulder. It felt so right. "I know I shouldn't, but I do. I think about the lie I told." Then she told him about her anxiety issues, about the panic attacks, and the phobias. He just hugged her tighter. He kissed the side of her face, right at the temple.

"I don't care about that." He stopped and was silent a beat. "I do care, but I know you'll work it out. You always do."

"Yeah, I've got a plan, and I'm doing good. I just have to accept myself for who I am and not try to be somebody…"

"Oh please, honey, stay who you are! I love you. Who cares if you're a little shy in large groups? Think I didn't know that?"

"Really? You did?" She pretended to smack his arm. "You never said."

"Lots of stuff I never said. Eighteen years worth. I'll start making up for all that time right now if you'll say yes."

Courtney didn't know what she was supposed to

agree to, and Edward must have seen that on her face. "I'm not saying let's get married or anything like that."

"Oh." She felt a pang.

"Because we're already married. You forget?" He lifted her chin and their gazes locked.

"The papers…"

"Never sent. Let's burn 'em."

She felt sweet relief rush through her.

"I want to be married to you forever."

"Me too. I want that, too." She did, more than anything.

"There's just one thing."

"What's that?"

"Could I have that dining room there as a music room, maybe with a television and a leather chair for watching the game?"

"What game?" She wondered when he was planning on moving in.

"Oh, there's always a game. Tigers. Red Wings. Pistons. Lions." He paused. "Unless you want to move into the glass house?"

"No. It's too small for three."

"Well, then let me lease you an office in town because this place is too small for clients who may have issues."

Wow. Whoa. She hadn't even gotten that far yet.

"We can take it slow. I won't order the leather chair until you feel like you want me here."

She didn't care about holding in anything anymore. She jumped on his lap and kissed him on the mouth. They kissed a long time, and then she said, "Stay." And he did.

A word about the author...

Prolific author Cynthia Harrison edges closer to mystery with this third in a series featuring a lakeside tourist town in Northern Michigan.

Harrison has been published widely in print, penning poetry, book reviews for top trade magazines, and short memoirs in anthologies. Her essays on writing and other topics have appeared online since 2002 at www.cynthiaharrison.com.

A former creative writing teacher at her local community college, Harrison wrote her first book (and her only non-fiction title) for her students.

http://www.cynthiaharrison.com

Thank you for purchasing
this publication of The Wild Rose Press, Inc.

If you enjoyed the story, we would appreciate your
letting others know by leaving a review.

For other wonderful stories,
please visit our on-line bookstore at
www.thewildrosepress.com.

For questions or more information
contact us at
info@thewildrosepress.com.

The Wild Rose Press, Inc.
www.thewildrosepress.com

Stay current with The Wild Rose Press, Inc.

Like us on Facebook

https://www.facebook.com/TheWildRosePress

And Follow us on Twitter
https://twitter.com/WildRosePress

Made in the USA
San Bernardino, CA
11 February 2016